HIS THRE
SUI⟩

A BEDROOM SECRETS SERIES

EMMA THORNE

CHAPTER 1

I never was one of those boy crazy girls. In high school, instead of mooning over the football players, I ran track through the hills of eastern Washington, always pushing myself to be faster and stronger than everyone else including my three older brothers.

Instead of wringing my hands worrying about which boy was going to ask me to the Homecoming Dance, I worked in dad's orchards, picking apples by hand to keep that year's harvest from spoiling after a bad hail storm.

And then I met Troy.

When I was eighteen years old, we kissed beneath the branches of an apple tree during a rainstorm. Our lips touched and I understood that I'd never been kissed before.

Troy's kiss made my toes curl and set butterflies a flight in my belly. Troy's kiss lit a fire in my body in places I didn't even know existed.

He was my first for everything.

My first kiss.

My first love.

I may have waited until I was eighteen years old to go boy crazy, but once I fell in love with Troy Van Rossum all bets were off. I was out of my mind with desire. I believed that all we needed was each other until the day that Troy changed his mind.

He left town without a word and I never heard from him again.

For ten years I buried my pain, put on a brave face and tried to avoid the ghost of us in my hometown. I moved away and moved on. I told myself that I was over him. I told myself the past was the past and I'd been a fool to trust a man like him with my tender heart.

I almost believed my own lies.

The trouble with running from the truth is sooner or later your past comes back to town throwing punches and next thing you know you're slapping people in the face.

Well, that may not happen to everyone but it happened to me and this is how it all went down.

CHAPTER 2

Bleary eyed and buzzed from chain drinking black coffee, I pulled into the parking lot of Salishan General Hospital. It was 2:00 a.m., and my hometown was asleep. Stars glittered overhead in the night sky. An icy fog hovered above the asphalt. Some might have called it peaceful, but the quiet made me uneasy.

Right then, it was shameful but truthful, I wished I were sound asleep in my bed at the Holiday back in Seattle. I didn't want to be here, I didn't want to come home, but I'd had no choice.

I hugged my arms as I climbed out of the car into the biting air.

The only people up at this time on a weeknight were drunks rolling home after last call and people like me who wished they weren't visiting someone they loved in the hospital.

Mom's voice had woken me from a deep sleep with a shot of adrenaline that still hadn't faded. "Come home Shea Marie. It's Daddy. We need you." I hadn't called my father *Daddy* since I was a little girl and the truth was things had never been the same between us since that pivotal summer, ten years ago.

Emma Thorne

I closed my eyes and exhaled for a moment standing beneath a yellowed streetlamp in the parking lot. After all this time, the memory of Dad's disappointment in me still made it hard for me to breathe. Damn I hated how every time I set foot in my hometown the old feelings of guilt and shame spooled up as if I were that brokenhearted eighteen-year-old all over again.

Dad was in the hospital and my family needed me, so I'd rescheduled all my clients for the week. I'd left a note for my best friend, Odessa, so she wouldn't worry when I was a no show for our morning run. My life was officially on hold, at least for a few days.

I'd gotten pretty good at coming up with reasons not to come home over the last ten years, but this wasn't a family barbecue or a holiday where I could buzz in and out without staying the night.

Standing in the parking lot, I pulled my cell phone out of my purse and called my older brother Caiden. The last time I'd been in this hospital I'd been eleven years old with a broken arm after jumping out of an apple tree on a dare. Now I was twenty-eight, exhausted from driving all night and nothing looked familiar.

"Where are you?" Caiden answered, picking up quickly.

"Here," I said, walking towards the ER. "Where are you?"

"Wait in the parking lot," Caiden said. Then I heard a rustling sound like he'd muffled the phone with his hand. People were shouting.

I stopped in my tracks. "What's going on in there?"

"Stay there," Caiden said. "Hey Max, grab him. Grab him!"

Caiden and Max were identical twins and I was used to them causing trouble but this seemed off even for them. "What are you two . . .?

"It's not a good time little sister."

I hated being reminded of my rank.

"Not a good time?" I said, picking up my pace and heading straight for the double doors to the emergency room. "Of course it's not a good time. Dad's had a heart attack."

"Stay where you are. Trust me on this one Shea."

"I'm coming in."

"Just wait . . ."

"I'm coming in Caiden!" I shouted, heading for the entrance. The fact that I didn't know where I was going occurred to me but I'd just driven all night, fueled by fear that Dad might die before sunrise and now my twin brothers were in some sort of a brawl and wanted me to stay in the parking lot? Hell no.

The doors to the ER swished open and the question of where to find my brothers was quickly answered.

"You son of a bitch!" a voice I recognized shouted.

"Ben?" I said. I'd know my oldest brother's I'm-going-to-kick-your-ass-voice anywhere. Sure enough, I looked over just in time to see Ben lower his shoulder and ram smack in the middle of a tall guy in a black suit in the middle of the empty lobby.

"Stay away from us!" Ben shouted as he wrestled the suit to the floor. They seemed to be pretty evenly matched. Ben kept throwing air punches as the other guy rolled away just in time, he wasn't fighting back. The suit was clearly more into dodging then throwing.

"I'm calling the police!" The nurse at the desk shouted, cradling a phone against her ear. I recognized her in flash. It was Mrs. Ingram our old next door neighbor. I'd grown up side by side with her son, Paul. "Hey sweetie!" She said, her face lighting up for a moment as she saw me.

"I am the police," Caiden said, flashing his badge. He moved closer to the fight trying to get a good angle on either of the parties. "I got this Mrs. Ingram, stand down." Caiden had one of those charming, smooth voices that sounded like sweet talk even when shouting. "Max! Get in here and help me out!"

Max was two minutes older than Caiden but years behind him in maturity. He was also a surgeon and deathly afraid of hurting his precious hands. Max grimaced and tried to move in making a half-hearted attempt to get into the mix.

"Oh for God's sake," I said, placing two fingers between my lips. I wasn't physically stronger than my brothers but one thing I'd learned being the youngest in a family of boys is the person with the shrillest whistle usually won. "Knock it off!" I shouted. Then I took a deep breath and blew.

"What in the Christ . . ." Ben jumped to his feet holding his ears.

Caiden and Max looked at me, both clutching their heads as I continued to blow.

The guy in the suit curled up on himself his back towards me.

"All right?" I said, finally stopping to look at my brothers. "What the hell is going on here?"

Caiden breathed a sigh of relief. "Never mind. I got this," he said.

"Do you really officer," I said, not bothering to hide

my sarcasm. Caiden knelt down beside the man on the floor, offering him a hand.

"I didn't need your help," Ben said, staggering towards me. His black hair sweaty, he looked red-faced and wild-eyed. Caiden, Max, and I took after Mom with her pale skin and strawberry blonde curls, while Ben had always been the spitting image of our dark eyed father. He'd also inherited his temper and Ben was no stranger to the drink. I could smell the alcohol on him from a few feet away.

"Seems like you do need my help," I said, waving my hand in front of my nose. "Seriously, Dad is sick and you're acting like you're in a bar fight at the hospital."

"Right," Ben said, sneering. "Fine time for you to lecture me on putting your family first."

"I'm here now, Ben, give it a rest," I said, knowing I already had my backup. This was why coming home was so hard for me. I could never make it through a visit without someone reminding me of my mistakes, past, present, and doomed to happen future.

"Why don't you take Shea upstairs to see Mom?" Caiden said nodding to Max.

"No," Ben said, grabbing Max's arm. "I think she should see her old friend first don't you?" Ben grinned and crossed his arms nodding towards the man on the floor.

"Come on, Ben," Max said, looking uncomfortable. "Let's go upstairs, Shea."

"What friend?" I looked past Caiden. I'd been so distracted by my brothers I'd almost forgotten about Ben's unfortunate dance partner.

In front of a row of empty waiting room chairs, the man in the black suit pulled himself to his feet. His back turned to me he brushed off the legs of his trousers.

I froze.

An old friend?

I knew him.

I knew those hands.

I knew that body.

I stared at the cut of his shoulders, the shape of his neck as he looked to the side. I'd touched his naked skin in the dark with our legs tangled together. I'd felt the thrill of his fingers running through my hair.

Suddenly I was aware of nothing but my heartbeat, nothing but my breath. The temperature in the waiting room felt ten degrees warmer.

"You know I can check that eye out for you," Max said moving between us trying to run interference. He lifted the man's chin slightly holding it up in the light. "I don't even think you'll have a black eye my friend."

"I'm fine, thank you." The man stepped away from Max right into my line of sight.

"Hello Shea," he said.

My knees about buckled. I reached out and steadied myself on a chair.

It had been ten years since I'd seen his face, but I would have recognized those bright blue eyes and sweet smile anywhere. His hair was still thick and chocolate brown, the dimple in his left cheek unchanged. He looked older and rugged with a five o'clock shadow dusting his jaw.

Long ago he'd been the cowboy of my dreams wearing flannel, denim, and steel toe boots just like my brothers. In a tailored black suit, a crisp white button down, vest and tie, it was clear he wasn't from anywhere close to around here.

Damn. He still looked good. He looked hot and disheveled and all of a sudden I was struggling against the urge to throw my arms around the neck of Troy Van Rossum, the boy who had broken my heart.

* * * *

"It's been a while," Troy said. His cheeks flushed from the fight, his blue eyes looked bright and he smiled despite

14

the red swelling on his cheek.

"Nice three-piece suit," I said, unable to think of anything else to say. I held onto the back of that chair for dear life causing my knuckles to turn white.

"It's good to see you," he said, smiling at me as if we were the only two people in the room.

His smile unlocked a summer of memories, they flashed in front of me like the pages of a book turning.

His shy smile, the day we'd met in the orchard.

Our first kiss, the way his lips felt fluttering against mine, the touch of his hand on the back of my neck.

Three flashes of light through my bedroom window, it had been our signal to find each other, our code for I love you, and I had believed him every time.

I felt the weight of Caiden, Max, and Ben's stare. Even Mrs. Ingram seemed stunned into silence. I suppose everyone was asking the same question.

What would Shea Marie O'Toole do to the man who had abandoned her on the courthouse steps the day she was supposed to be his bride?

"You look good," Troy said.

And something about that comment snapped me back to reality like a rubber band snapping against my skin.

He broke his promise. He broke my heart. He lied.

Emma Thorne

After a decade of total silence, Troy Van Rossum had the gall to walk back into my life and give me a shallow compliment? You look good? I didn't look good. In fact, I was pretty sure I looked like I was in need of a hairbrush, a toothbrush, and a good night's sleep.

My body lit up with rage, ten full years of it.

"We should talk," he said.

"No thank you," I answered. And without hesitation, I strode right across that room and I slapped him in the face.

CHAPTER 3

What had I just done? I looked down at my palm, it was red and stinging. I felt as though I'd stepped outside my body. Had I really just slapped Troy in the face? This made no sense at all. Troy lived 3,000 miles away and he'd wiped his hands clean of me years ago. Why would he come back to Salishan? And why was he at the hospital tonight?

Troy's bright blue eyes locked on mine. "I deserved that," he said, his voice soft.

"I . . . I . . ." I wanted to say something, say anything, I had so many questions but my brain was spinning in circles and I felt dizzy with anger and another emotion that felt more like grief. "Troy?" I asked, my voice sounded small even to me.

"Jesus, Shea. That's enough." And just like that Caiden was beside me. I felt his strong hands on my arms as he spun me away from Troy and escorted me across the room.

I didn't resist as we weaved through rows of chairs stepping over Ben's splayed legs. He'd taken a seat on the carpet right by Mrs. Ingram's desk. She leaned over the counter holding a glass of water for him in her outstretched hand.

"Come by the house later honey," she called after me. "Paul will be so glad you're home."

"Thank you Mrs. Ingram," I stammered, stumbling forward.

I glanced back over my shoulder. Troy stood frozen in place, watching me. He held one hand to his jaw massaging his cheek. Max stood beside him talking. I imagined he was trying to do damage control. Max's voice was loud and bright. "You know I've been slapped a few times myself, this won't even leave a scar."

With his hand on my elbow, Caiden escorted me down a hall pointing me towards a bank of elevators. "I told you to wait outside," he said, using his police officer voice.

"Quit talking to me like I'm a criminal. I'm your sister."

"Then quit acting like a delinquent."

"No. Wait. Wait a minute," I said, slapping Caiden's hand off my arm as we reached the elevators. "What's he doing here?" I asked, pointing towards the waiting room. "That's Troy. He's back. What the hell Caiden." My eyes darting, heart racing, the realization I was awake and this was really happening felt like a punch in the gut.

"I know it's Troy," Caiden said, leaning in to press the up button and then rubbing his temple. "I told you to wait. I wanted to warn you, not have you walk into the middle of that shit show."

"I just slapped him in the face." I looked down at my hand. "I mean it felt good. It felt good to hit him. It felt really good, which is so wrong. It's been ten years, Caiden. Ten years. Who doesn't reach out for ten years?"

"Somebody that you hope doesn't feel like pressing charges," Caiden said, holding the doors open for me.

"Pressing charges!" My heart rate sky-rocketed. "He won't. He wouldn't dare."

"Well, it's my job to find out. Maybe you and Ben will get lucky tonight. I hope he's feeling generous." Caiden leaned inside and pressed the button for the fifth floor. "Turn right when you get out, Dad's in room 502. Please go straight there and don't cause any more trouble. Mom's upstairs alone."

"You still haven't explained to me—" The elevator doors closed.

* * * *

I stood in that elevator trying to breathe like a normal person. I had thought that rushing to my father's bedside in the middle of the night was going to be my biggest challenge. I had never in a million years thought I'd see the boy whose memory I'd been hiding from for so long.

I wished I could call Odessa. I needed to talk to

someone. I needed a stiff drink.

The elevator doors opened.

I turned just in time to see my Mom stick her head out into the hall from what must have been Dad's room. Her face lit up when she saw me.

I took a breath and smiled, putting on my best poker face. "Hey Mom," I said, trying to stand strong, telling myself that no good could come of telling Mom that Troy was downstairs. She was worried enough about Dad, and she didn't need to hear that two of her children had ended up throwing punches in the ER.

"Shea?" Mom asked closing the door behind her and walking towards me, her arms open wide. Seeing her kind eyes, I felt paper thin and blowing in the wind.

Tears poured down my face, hard and fast.

Mom hugged me tight her head pressing up against my shoulder. I have been taller than mom since eighth grade. Holding her always makes me feel like a little girl, pretending to be a grown-up and failing.

I knew she thought I was crying about Dad and I was. I was also crying for myself and my aching heart, I felt as though the thin stitches holding it together had been torn open with one glance from Troy.

They say time is supposed to heal you, but I clearly

hadn't healed. Here I was sobbing in my mother's arms the way I'd cried when Troy had left me without saying good-bye.

Less than thirty minutes home and I felt broken in two.

CHAPTER 4

Mom reached up to hold my face in her hands. "He's going to be fine honey," she said, smiling in spite of the tears sliding down her cheeks. "It's just scary. It's real scary for me too."

"Oh come on Mom, you can't start crying," I said, laughing as I wiped my cheeks with the heel of my hand. "If you start to cry, I am never going to stop." Mom and I were known for our co-sympathetic waterworks.

"I'm not crying," Mom said, wiping her eyes. She straightened up and rolled her shoulders back. "It's good to see you home. It's been a while honey. All my babies are back and I'm sorry but I get a little emotional."

How long had it been since I'd been home? I'd missed Christmas that year to travel after a big fitness conference in Vegas. It was an important event and Mom had seemed supportive of the idea. I did a quick inventory of the last few holidays. Fourth of July, nope. Easter, no. Thanksgiving. I inhaled sharply. I had let almost a full year go by without coming home.

Ben walked up behind us lips smacking as he chewed gum. "Is he awake?" He asked Mom, nodding at the door. On top of the gum, I smelled a big waft of minty mouthwash on his breath. Caiden and Max must have cleaned him up before sending him upstairs.

"Say hi to your sister, Benjamin," Mom said.

"We saw each other," Ben said.

"Downstairs," I said, looking at him, my lips pursed. "We saw each other downstairs, in the lobby."

"All right then," Mom said, looking at us both as if she knew we were keeping secrets.

"I've got some business I need to discuss with Dad," Ben said.

"Honey, don't stress him out."

"I won't," Ben said, slipping inside the room. Ben was the eldest and heir to the orchard. For as long as I remembered, it had always been understood that Ben would take over the family business. I suppose that was why the rest of us gravitated towards other careers. Caiden picked law enforcement, Max picked medicine, and I turned my love of running through the hills into a full time gig as a personal trainer.

"I'm sorry I've been away so much, Mom," I said.

"No apologies, you are a busy and successful girl. I'm proud of what you've accomplished in Seattle." Mom sniffed and smoothed back her wavy red hair. It was streaked with more thick bands of silver than I remembered.

Mom was always so beautiful to me, and I admired how she refused to dye her hair. She could afford to but couldn't stomach paying someone for something so frivolous.

Caiden stepped out of the elevator followed by Max. If it weren't for their different clothes, it would be easy to get the two of them confused. They had pulled that trick on girls in high school more than once I was ashamed to say.

I intercepted them in the hall before they got too close to Mom.

"Everything okay downstairs?" I asked.

"Yes," Caiden answered, keeping his voice low. "Troy's not pressing charges against either of you."

Hearing Troy's name again, my chest tightened and I waved my hands in front of my face beating back another wave of tears. "Sorry," I whispered. "I am an emotional mess. Thanks for taking care of everything."

"No worries," Caiden said, kissing the side of my head. "Now let's go see the old man."

We both heard the sound of shouting at the same time. We darted inside the room to find Ben standing arms crossed at the foot of Dad's bed.

Dad was trying to raise himself up, his face red from the effort. "You tell those sons of bitches that they can take their Goddamn offer and shove it up their suit wearing asses." Dad may have been recovering from a heart attack, but his voice sounded the same, gruff and booming. He sighed and collapsed back on his pillow. The moment he stopped yelling his color faded. I was shocked at the sight of his pale skin, it looked almost grey in the light.

"Dad, I just told you," Max said, moving to his bedside. "Less stress, not more . . . Come on Ben." He gave our oldest brother a gentle push.

I noticed how Ben stumbled, but I wasn't sure if Mom or Dad could tell that he was two sheets to the wind. I assumed that Ben's fight with Troy had something to do with Dad's command to stick the offer up their suit wearing asses. I had a thousand questions for my brothers about Troy, but I needed to remember the real reason I was home. He was sitting in a hospital bed right in front of me.

"Hey Dad," I whispered, moving towards the bed. "I hear you gave everyone a real scare today."

"Oh for Christ sake," Dad said, lifting a hand. "Mary you didn't need to call Shea. I'm not dying. I just had a little spell and these goddamn doctors think they know everything. I need to get back to work."

"And it sounds like you are feeling better," I said, plastering a smile on my face and giving Max and Caiden a look.

Caiden rolled his eyes and stared at the ceiling. Max just shook his head.

"I'm fine," Dad said. "I don't need all of you kids crowding around acting like I'm about to give up the ghost."

"Well, I'm happy to see you acting like your old self," I said, reaching down to give Dad an awkward hug. He squeezed me back, but I could sense he didn't have the strength that he used to. His eyes looked dim and his hair more salt than pepper.

Caiden motioned for us all to go outside. He had Ben by the elbow. Once again, he was trying to corral the family. Caiden was the perpetual peacemaker.

"Honey, we are going to let you rest a bit," Mom said. When she leaned down to kiss my dad, he reached up and stroked her cheek. I caught my breath. It was such a tender gesture, small but filled with so much love.

My father could be a bear. He could be scary, he could be brash, and he'd never quite forgiven me for what happened that summer with Troy. But I never doubted how much he loved our family, or the love he held for our mother.

He could be trusted unlike the man I'd chosen. I'd be more careful the next time I gave my heart away.

* * * *

26

His Three Piece Suit

I followed Mom and the boys down the hall to a small waiting room with a view of the hillside. Outside, I-90 cut across the landscape with a steady stream of headlights starting their early morning commute. The sun had started to rise painting the clouds with streaks of orange and pink.

Max put some quarters into an instant coffee maker machine which spat out a Styrofoam cup of something that smelled faintly of coffee.

"How bad is it?" I said, taking a seat in a maroon colored easy chair across from Mom and Ben. Caiden remained standing leaning against the wall, one hand always on his holster.

"The coffee?" Max said, taking a sip. "It's terrible, definitely not up to Seattle standards."

"No, Dad," I said, rolling my eyes.

"Oh, that," Max said, taking a seat. "Thanks to Mom, Dad got to the ER before there was any scarring or real damage done to his heart. They were able to treat the blockage with drugs instead of surgery. We'll know for sure over the next few days if he's dodged the surgery bullet."

"Surgery," I said, stretching my legs out and closing my eyes for a moment. "Oh my God, Dad hates doctors. No offense Max."

"None taken," Max said. "I'm pretty sure that Dad believes I'm part witch doctor the way he second guesses everything I tell him."

"Your dad is proud of you," Mom said, swatting my brother.

"Kidding mom," Max said. Mom was so literal when it came to protecting our hearts. "The thing is, even if Dad avoids surgery this is a wake-up call for him. He is going to need some PT to strengthen his lungs and his back. He took a fall today when he collapsed. He needs to simplify his life, eat well, work out, and minimize stress."

"None of that sounds like Dad," Caiden said.

"Simplify," Ben snorted. "If he wants a stress-free life, he should get this family out of the orchard business."

"Benjamin," Mom said, turning her attention to her oldest son. "Are you ready to tell us what you and Dad were discussing in his room?"

"Just business," Ben said, leaning back, arms crossed. "Dad and I have got things under control."

"I see," Mom said, not pressing. I wondered if she ever got tired of being told that the orchard wasn't her business. It drove me crazy and I hadn't been home in a year.

Mom fixed her gaze on me. "Okay then. How about one of you kids tell me why Troy Van Rossum is back in town?"

"How do you know this stuff?" I said. Then I glared at Caiden and Max. "How does Mom know Troy's downstairs and I didn't."

"Downstairs?" Mom said, eyebrows rising. "I didn't know that."

"Well, don't look at me," I said. "I didn't know he was back until I walked into the lobby to see Ben punching him."

"Punching him," Mom said.

"Shea," Caiden sighed.

"Well, why didn't any of you tell me he was home?" I gasped. "How long have you all known."

No one said a word for a moment.

Caiden spoke first. "Troy's been back about six months."

"Six months," I jumped to my feet. "Six months and none of you thought to tell me."

"You haven't been around little sister," Ben said.

I hated that he was right. I sank back down into my chair.

"Besides I don't think lover boy came back for you," Ben continued.

"What's that supposed to mean," I said, glaring at him.

"Troy works for Ardent Ventures," Max said.

"What is that? Is that supposed to mean something to me?" I asked.

"They are an investment firm based in New York that focuses on vacation property development," Max shrugged. "What? I googled them, all right?"

"What does Ardent Ventures want in Salishan?" I asked.

"To steal our fucking orchards," Ben said, red-faced.

"Ben!" Mom said.

"Really. He wants the orchards," I said, not buying any of this. I felt like Ben had bought into some big city conspiracy theory. "Why would Troy want our land? He has money and he left. He left Salishan and he never looked back."

"People like him are never satisfied with what they have. He may have money, but I guarantee you that he is back here for more," Ben said. "He's a greedy, opportunistic—"

"Look, the truth is we don't know why he is here," Caiden interrupted. "We haven't exactly had Troy over for dinner and explored his motivations."

"Well, I wouldn't expect that," I said. "It just makes no sense. We're not selling right?"

"Damn right we are not," Ben said.

Finally, something we agreed on.

"All right then," I said, standing. "We tell him no. And then he leaves town. This isn't complicated people."

"I've already told him no," Ben said.

"So, why is he still here?"

"I told you. He's a liar," Ben said. "The orchard is doing just fine. We don't need anyone's help."

"What do you mean we don't need help?" I asked. "You make no sense."

"He was a lying piece of shit ten years ago when he kicked you to the curb," Ben said.

"Hey, I remember what he did to me. I don't need you acting like a deranged asshole to remind me of my broken heart, thank you very much."

"Oh, so I'm the deranged asshole."

"When did you get so angry?" I asked Benjamin, my chest shaking.

"Enough! Both of you, mind your manners," Mom said, her tone biting. She looked at Ben and me with the same hard stare she'd used when reminding us that she expected us to be quiet in church or to put our dishes in the dishwasher instead of stacking them in the sink.

"Sorry Mom," I said, closing my eyes. I felt exhausted and stupid for allowing Ben to bait me into some sort of regressed teenage fight. Had Ben always been this jaded, or had I really been away too long? "

"It's late," Mom said, standing. "You kids go home now."

"Mom I came to help you," I said.

"Just seeing your beautiful face is a help," Mom said. "You've had a few shocks tonight, first Dad and now Troy. Go home, eat some pie, sleep in your old room. You can take a shift tomorrow. I want to know that my baby girl is rested and well fed."

"Mom, you know I feed myself on a pretty regular basis in Seattle."

"What? Cocktails and appetizers? I love Odessa but the girl does not know how to cook a proper meal. You need your mother and don't you ever forget it."

I wasn't going to argue with her about that.

"Let's go," Caiden said, taking my arm. "You too Ben. I'll drop you off at Mom and Dad's."

"I thought you were living with Daisy?" I asked, Ben. The moment the question left my mouth I wished I'd had the good sense to keep my mouth shut.

Ben held his mouth in a tight line for a moment before answering. "Broke up," he said. "For real this time."

"I see," I said. "I'm sorry Ben."

He wasn't listening. He'd already started down the hall with Caiden a few steps behind.

"All right, then good night," I said, hugging Mom and Max. I followed my brothers outside thinking about Ben's broken heart and Dad's near miss with death. These were good reminders that life was short and I wasn't the only person who had ever been hurt by love. It was time for me to really let go of the pain I'd been carrying for a decade. I needed to turn that slap into closure. It was time for me to act like a grown-up and not an angry teenage girl.

"Follow me home?" Caiden asked, before climbing into his police cruiser with Ben in the back seat.

"Sure thing," I said, my eyes scanning the parking lot for Troy before I was aware of what I was looking for. So much for letting go and being evolved. I was a hopeless case.

CHAPTER 4

As I followed Caiden and Ben out of the parking lot I fought the urge to pull a U-turn and take I-90 straight home to Seattle. I felt weak for even being tempted but coming home was hard. Dad was still angry and as usual didn't seem happy to see me. I supposed he was mad I'd stayed away for so long. I wasn't sure he'd ever really forgiven me for moving away. And talking to Ben was like looking for sanity inside a fireball of rage. It occurred to me that he might be angrier at Troy than me.

Troy.

To be honest, he was the real reason I wanted to leave. It had taken me years to accept that he wasn't coming back ever. He wasn't allowed to come home after all this time. It was against the rules. Didn't he know that?

"You can't break the rules," I gasped pounding the steering wheel as I drove.

It was still early. Traces of the hot pink sunrise lingered in the sky. I wanted to call my best friend, Odessa, but I wasn't sure she'd be awake yet. I craved hearing a voice from my real life on the other side of the mountains where nobody knew about my past with Troy. I'd been away from the Holiday in Seattle for less than twenty-four hours and already I felt as if I'd lost some part of myself on the journey here.

I didn't feel strong here, I felt heartbroken and out of control.

Odessa understood heartbreak. Her boyfriend Marco, had died in a terrible helicopter accident, something, I reminded myself, that should give me some perspective.

I had no real problems. Dad was going to recover and Ben was mad at me, but so what? The orchard wasn't for sale. Troy would get his answer and leave . . . again.

What was my biggest problem? I'd had my heart broken at age eighteen? So what. I needed to toughen up. Odessa had watched the love of her life plummet into the sea right before her very eyes and she was still standing.

I needed to dig deep and pull myself together. I was here to help my family, not throw a pity party for my teenage dreams.

The clock in my car changed to 5:30 a.m. Maybe Odessa was awake. Idling at a stop light I sent a quick text, careful that Caiden didn't see. In his current mood, he might just write me up a ticket.

You awake?

My phone rang right away.

"Hello," I answered on speaker.

"You checking to make sure I'm still alive, or that I remember to go to work or both?" Odessa said, sounding groggy but happy to hear from me.

"Both and I'm calling to tell you to go for a run," I said. "It's a great way to start your day, wake up your muscles, wake up your mind."

"Thanks personal trainer," she said.

"You're welcome," I said, forcing a smile. "It's good to hear your voice. It is so weird being home."

"How is your dad?" Odessa asked. "You sound stressed."

"I'm good. Dad's good," I said, hoping if I said it enough I'd sound believable. "Dad had a heart attack but so far they think no damage, and looks like he's going to avoid surgery. Mom got him to the doctor in time, which is a minor miracle."

"That is lucky," Odessa said, sounding more alert. "How is your mom holding up?"

"She's good," I said, driving passing Salishan high school, the Teddy Bear day care and an Auto Parts store where the boys worked in the summer. Things in this town never seemed to change. "Everyone is okay more or less."

"What do you mean more or less, you sound weird."

"So, how do I explain this," I said. "My older brother

Ben just got drunk and punched the boy who broke my heart ten years ago and then I slapped him. I mean I slapped the boy who broke my heart, not my brother."

"Wait, which boy?"

"I haven't told you much about him," I said. "It's embarrassing."

"What do you mean embarrassing?"

"It was the summer before my senior year of high school. I met Troy Van Rossum and we were crazy in love." My voice caught. I exhaled as I turned down the long driveway that led to my parent's house. Caiden was heading up the drive having dropped Ben off already. He flashed his lights at me as he passed.

"So he was your high school sweetheart," Odessa said.

"He was more than that," I said, parking the car in front of the house. "We were engaged. I almost married him."

"In high school?" I couldn't see Odessa but from her tone, I knew her eyes were wide and I had her full attention.

"He asked me to marry him and I said yes. I was eighteen."

"Oh my God, what happened? I can't believe you never told me about this."

I closed my eyes and exhaled. "I waited for Troy all

day at the courthouse. I sat there in a white sundress until they locked the doors. Troy never came. My friend Paul showed up to drive me home or I think I would have been there all night. I didn't believe it. I still don't sometimes."

"He left you there," Odessa said.

"Stood me up and I never heard from him again."

"Until now."

"Yep," I said, opening my eyes, blinking back tears.

"So, let me see if I understand this. You have given me a lot to process. I need coffee. Are you sure you didn't make this all up to try and distract me from my train wreck of a life?"

"I'm afraid not."

"All right then," she said. I could tell from her voice she was in the kitchen of her new apartment. She'd recently rented a one bedroom with her new roommate, an artist named Theo Manhattan, who sure looked like boyfriend material to me. He was certainly hot enough, but Odessa swore up and down there were just friends.

"Your old love shows up after breaking your heart, I totally get why you slapped him. What was up with your brother? You said Ben was drunk and he punched him? Was he defending your honor?"

"Ben claims that Troy is trying to steal my Dad's farm

out from under him which is crazy because it's not for sale."

"Holy shit." Odessa said. She was definitely awake now. She sipped her coffee. "Your life is basically a super bad country song."

"You don't even listen to country music, Odessa," I said, laughing. I was suddenly so grateful for her friendship and humor.

"God no," she said. "I think I hate country music. I don't really know because I won't listen to it, but, I have an excellent imagination and your life is exactly how I imagine a bad country song. Do you need me to rescue you? Show up in the middle of the night and drag you back to civilization?"

"No, I'm okay," I said, sighing. "I'm here for my family and I'm not going to let my lying ex-fiancé drive me away."

"I'm sorry," she said. "You must be so tired, hon."

I looked out the window at my parent's house. It was a classic two story yellow and white farmhouse complete with a big red barn. It looked the same as always, but everything was different. Mom and Dad were at the hospital, Ben was apparently back at home and somewhere in the town of Salishan, Troy was either waking up or going to sleep. "None of this seems real," I said.

"I know the feeling," Odessa said. She didn't need to tell me she was thinking about Marco.

"I'm sorry I never told you about Troy before. This must all sound so silly and self-absorbed to you."

"You loved him hon," Odessa said.

"Ten years ago."

"But he was your first love," she said.

"Yes he was."

"First loves never end very cleanly. I'm not sure I believe they ever end at all. They change the shape of your heart, they make you the person you are."

"You are right about that," I said, nodding and biting back a surprising batch of tears. Troy had influenced so many of my choices, where I lived, how often I came home. My life was covered in his fingerprints and he hadn't laid a hand on me in a decade. "I just needed to talk to you and remind myself of my life, of who I am when I'm not here."

"Oh, I can remind you," Odessa said. I imagined her standing in the middle of her apartment, her shoulders thrown back, her head held high. "You are Shea Marie O'Toole, one of the most highly paid and sought after personal trainers in Seattle." Odessa's voice grew stronger with every word. "You are an entrepreneur. A business woman. A force of nature. You take shit from no one and are taking names in life. Now say it with me. You take shit . . ."

I started to laugh.

"I take shit from no one."

We spoke in unison.

"I take shit from no one and am taking names in life."

"Good girl," she said.

"Thank you," I said, taking a breath. I looked at the miles of apple trees on the sloping hillside behind our house. I could make out the dirt trail where I'd pounded out a thousand different emotions through the years.

"Now go take names," Odessa said. "I've got your back. Go sleep."

"Nah, I know what I need to do," I said, getting out of the car and grabbing my duffle from the trunk. "I'm going for a run." My legs itched to tear open that road.

* * * *

I dropped my duffle in my old bedroom. Mom had kept the same flowered bedspread and hadn't re-papered the room, but she had moved in her sewing machine and a Nordic Track which meant it was pretty crammed. I knew why she picked this spot to work out. On the second floor, my room had the best view of the orchard.

I stood at the window and looked outside remembering

the nights Troy had stood outside my bedroom flashing the pen light he kept on his keychain three times.

One. Two. Three.

"Three times for three words," he'd said, pulling me in close for a kiss.

"Three words?" I'd answered my heart pounding.

"I. Love. You."

It was our shared secret. I'd always believed in the magic of the number with three, but Troy and I took it's meaning to the next level.

Three flashes of headlights, three coins on a table, three lines on a chalkboard, three apples sitting in a row on a stone wall.

I blinked. The past was gone.

The boy who had stood outside my window was all grown-up and sleeping somewhere with a closet full of shiny black suits.

I changed into my work out gear and laced up my running shoes, pulled my hair up into a ponytail, and put my cellphone in my jacket pocket.

I walked down the hall past Ben's room.

The door closed, I wondered if my brother was sleeping off his anger. I was about to knock but thought better of it. I needed to take care of myself first, my own emotions were difficult enough to manage. I couldn't handle Ben's anger, not yet.

I went down the stairs two at a time and headed out the backdoor. Screen door slamming, I took off running down the path fast and hard. The ground felt good and familiar. This trail had been one of my big escapes as a girl and I felt the same about it now. It was the perfect distraction. Every step a little uneven, I had to concentrate on my feet to keep from stumbling.

With every step, I reminded myself of who I was.

Shea O'Toole.

A strong woman.

With every step, I felt myself digging in deeper to my sense of self.

I didn't need Troy.

I was strong.

I hadn't needed Troy for years.

I was powerful.

Troy had disappeared without a trace and that was fine by me.

I was no longer a sad young girl with a broken heart.

I didn't want him any longer.

I didn't want to be his wife.

The path sloped up slightly as the rows of apple trees

climbed a small hill. I passed the valley where Troy and I used to meet. It had been the perfect hiding place; I'd always felt like we were a million miles away from the world.

And it didn't matter anymore.

Troy was no longer in my life.

I crested the hill and zigzagged down into the valley mixing it up by going off the trail and pushing myself even harder.

Troy was a memory.

A bad dream.

I glanced up in time to see someone step out of the trees directly into my path.

"Hey!" I had no hope of avoiding a collision. We crashed together tumbling onto the ground a pile of arms and legs.

When I opened my eyes, I was lying directly on top of Troy Van Rossum.

"Hello again," he said, smiling with that damn dimple looking so sweet and hot.

"What in the hell?" I gasped rolling off of him and jumping to my feet.

"Don't hit me again," he said, getting up quickly. He still had on his black suit, but instead of looking rumpled, he just looked sexy and disheveled. Damn him.

"Why shouldn't I hit you again?" I asked, pacing. "And it was a slap. I just slapped you."

"Shea, I'm here to say I'm sorry," he said. The red welt from his fight from Ben had turned slightly purple over the last few hours.

"Well, that's nice but I heard you at the hospital and you're a little late," I said. I glanced at him trying not to linger too long on his face. Sunlight glinted on the sexy stubble covering his cheeks bathing him in a golden light. He was more gorgeous out here in the trees, away from the buzzing fluorescent lights at the hospital.

The truth was that the years had done the boy I had loved good. I could still see the face of my young lover, but time had taken away some of his softness. He looked strong and lean. His cheekbones and jaw were chiseled, and I'd felt how strong his body was when we'd landed on the grass. The man was cut.

"You still don't know how to dress in an orchard," I said, surprised to hear myself making a joke about the night we'd met. Troy had crashed an orchard kegger, wearing khaki pants and a button down shirt. He could not have been more out of place.

"You're right about that," Troy said smiling and taking

a step toward me. "I am so sorry about what happened at the hospital with your brother."

"Ben says you're trying to force Dad to sell the orchards when they aren't for sale." I watched his face for a reaction. "Is that true?"

"It's more complicated than that," he said. "I'm trying to help your family. The orchard is financially," he paused as if searching for the right word, "vulnerable."

"Vulnerable? Is this your opinion as a potential buyer?"

"It's not like that Shea."

"My family's finances are none of your business," I said, my heart thumping in double time. I felt a fire in my belly as if I were a mama bear protecting my cubs.

"I'm sorry, I don't mean to suggest . . ." He looked pained and ran a hand through his dark brown hair.

"You did mean to talk about my family," I said. I walked towards him fighting the voice in my mind that told me the safest place for my heart was miles away from this man. "It's been a long time, Troy. You don't get to show up in my life, punch my brother . . ."

"To be fair, he punched me."

"Whatever. You don't get to fight with my family and then ambush me out here, in the place where we . . ." my voice caught and a shock of heat rolled through my body as tears filled my eyes. "Damn you," I whispered stopping myself.

"This is where we used to meet," Troy said, his voice soft. He moved closer. Sunlight had warmed the morning and a soft breeze blew through the trees. "I thought you might come here. I remember how it used to help you think. I remember everything, Shea."

"You don't get to talk to me about this place anymore," I whispered, my legs locked in place, my vision blurring with tears.

"This is where I loved you Shea".

I opened my mouth to speak but my mind was wiped clean by the image of his face, by the heat of his body inching closer.

"I loved you and you loved me," he said.

"I don't love you anymore," I whispered, looking up into his eyes. Troy was so close. Hands at his side he stood in that gorgeous black suit that was so out of place in this wild country.

"I made so many mistakes," he whispered lowering his head towards mine but stopping short of touching me.

"Damn right you did," I said.

"I'm going to make up for all of them."

"You can't," I whispered.

"Give me a chance," he said, then he lifted my chin with his fingertips, his touch felt electric. My mind was racing telling me to push him away, telling me to run but my heart wanted nothing but this, nothing but him.

"Let me try," he whispered. Then he kissed me and it was like a lightning bolt went through my body. My heart split open and all of the memories I'd locked up tight spilled out of my mind and filled my body with longing and need.

His lips pressed against mine.

I remembered the way he'd held my hand as we walked in the dark together.

His tongue slid into my mouth.

I remembered the feeling of our bodies slick with sweat. The way he'd looked at me the first time we gave ourselves to each other completely.

His hands pressed on my lower back.

I remembered the last time we'd made love in the orchard. We made a plan. I wrote a note saying good-bye to my family. I packed my bag.

A horn honked and I pushed Troy away, my heart pounding against my rib cage.

"You need to go," I gasped, struggling to catch my breath. He had made me wet with one kiss. Damn him.

His Three Piece Suit

Up on the hillside I caught a glimpse of a blue truck that I didn't recognize. Someone idled on the ridge. They had obviously seen us.

"Can I see you later?" Troy said, stepping away from me.

"No. No, you can't. That kiss. That was just sentimental. I shouldn't have done that."

"I'm glad you did."

"Troy, you can't just walk back into my life like nothing happened," I said. "My father is sick. I'm here to focus on him, not rekindle an old high school crush. Please stay away from me."

I said it to hurt him. I wanted to take it back the moment the words left my mouth, but another part of me enjoyed seeing him cringe.

"I see," Troy said. He nodded and bit his lip. "I'll go."

As I watched Troy walk away I told myself he was leaving for good. I wondered how he'd remembered the path to this place from the road. He'd been gone for so long.

He looked so out of place in his black suit weaving back and forth on the switchback out of the orchard, that is until he reached his sleek silver car parked at the back gate. I'd allowed myself to believe that he had the heart of this countryside in his soul, that he could find happiness with a girl like me.

Watching him climb into his shiny car wearing his three-piece suit, I didn't need Ben to tell me how wrong we were for each other. It had been a mistake to love him back then. I wasn't going to let him trick me again.

* * * *

The car on the ridge honked again.

"All right, all right," I yelled, taking a breath I sprinted up the hill. The burn in my legs felt good. It was definitely a distraction from the heat that had sprung up between my legs when Troy kissed me.

How had I allowed that to happen? I wondered running to the blue truck on the ridge. On closer look it was an old Ford with rusted paint and an engine that needed a tune up from the sound of it. I recognized that truck. It had parked in our driveway almost daily in high school.

The driver side door opened and out stepped my old friend, Paul Ingram.

"Hey, stranger," he said, holding his arms out for a hug. "Mom said you were back." Paul was tall with reddish brown hair and skin that freckled and turned golden brown over the summer.

"Hey," I said, grinning at him. I almost asked if she'd also told him that Troy was back in town and that my family had thrown down in the lobby of the hospital, but even though Paul had never told me, I knew that Troy was a sore spot between us. For years Paul and I had been best friends, and then I'd met Troy making Paul a third wheel who had never ever made it out of the friend box with me.

"Caiden said you'd be out here," he said.

"Seems everyone knows where I go to think."

"Shea, you ran like every day of high school. If he hadn't told me I would have guessed. I heard about your Dad, I'm sorry."

"Max thinks he's doing much better," I said, crossing my arms, my pulse still racing. Could Paul tell I'd just been making out with someone? Had he seen Troy leave? I was a grown woman so I know I shouldn't have cared, but I didn't really want to be called out especially by him. "Fingers crossed no surgery."

"Seems like things are turning around, I know its sure good to see you." He smiled. "Why'd you stop running? Don't you usually do a loop?"

I glanced back and realized that the spot where Troy had kissed me was partially obscured by the thick branches of a couple of trees. I'd made out with my ex-boyfriend and gotten away with it. I felt a mix of satisfaction and relief. "Oh, I'm tired from the drive. You want to head back to the house and catch up? Have a beer?"

"It's not even 7:00 a.m.," He said. "What has living in Seattle done to you, woman?"

"Oh, shut up," I said, giving him a playful shove. "Let's do coffee then."

"Or beer later, how'd you like to head into town and go to the Gold Digger for some drinks and darts tonight?"

"I don't know, my dad . . ." I said, knowing I sounded like I was making excuses. Somehow I felt I was always telling Paul no. I'd been telling this man no since we were kids.

"If he's still stable of course. I know why you've come home."

"I've been home before you know," I said.

"Yeah, but you never stay long, do you," he said, his voice a little softer.

I let his comment sit there, uncertain what to say. Paul smiled and looked at the clouds for a moment before grinning widely. "Come on, I'll drive you back unless you want to run it. Mom sent me with a coffee cake and a bunch of muffins too. She said you are too skinny."

"Seriously. What is it with our mother's and baked goods? They are trying to kill us with carbs."

"It's how they love us," he said. "You want a ride or

not?"

"Nah," I said, eyeing the road. "I'm going to run this one out. I'm going to finish it."

"All right then."

"But I'll take that coffee and that baked good when I've earned it." I pointed over the hillside. "Meet you back at the house in . . .seven minutes," I said, eyeing the path.

"That would be a pretty fast run."

"Seven minutes!" I shouted laughing, a rush of adrenaline racing through my body. "Ready, set, go!"

"See you Shea Marie!" Paul shouted after me as I took off down the trail.

Every step I repeated my mantra.

I am a strong woman.

I do not need Troy.

I am a powerful woman.

I do not want that man.

Taking no shit and taking names.

Right.

I spun a web of lies in my mind with every step I took.

When I got back to the house, Paul's truck was gone. I glanced down the drive and realized I was searching for Troy's silver car in the distance. Had I secretly been hoping that he'd ignored my protests and followed me home?

I was mental.

A plate of baked goods sat on the front porch with a note.

Gold Digger 8pm. See you tonight. P.

I held the note in my hand and exhaled.

I'd been avoiding going back to these old haunts for years. Hiding from the past no longer felt like a game I could play. The past had just walked into the orchard behind my house and kissed me. If I was going to ever feel comfortable coming home, I needed to face Troy and my memories, all of them, the good, the bad, and the scorching hot.

All of a sudden a beer full of courage did not seem like such a bad idea.

CHAPTER 5

The Gold Digger Restaurant and Bar is one block off the main drag of Salishan. The restaurant stands alone in a building that looks like a medium sized barn. Across the street is a line of storefronts that include La Fiesta Mexican Food, the pharmacy, and a video rental place that somehow stays in business.

The Gold Digger serves burgers and sweet potato fries and has a rotating tap of twelve beers, which makes it kind of a beer mecca with the young drinkers in town. It also rotates through a variety of apple themed dinners and desserts.

Pork chop with apple compote.

Chipotle burger and apple chips.

Spare Ribs and apple sauce.

If there is a way to add an apple, the people of Salishan will make it happen.

Against my better judgment I found myself sitting in the back of Caiden's police car right next to my brother Max, who was keeping us up to date on Dad's condition and also coordinating a late night hook up with one of his old flames.

"Dad's looking good, right?" He said, his face lit up

by the blue light of his phone as he texted. "He's responding very well to the blood thinners."

"I thought he still looked pale," I said. "I still think we should have made Mom go home for some rest," I said, feeling guilty about hitting the town.

"Put on the lights Cai," Max said.

Caiden didn't answer. He just ignored his slightly older brother.

"Mom wants us to go out and have fun, and Dad would lose his marbles if we all sat around wringing our hands and you know it," Max said. "Besides, I'm a really good doctor. The old man is going to pull through."

I rubbed my temples and glanced down at my outfit. I had on a pair of skinny jeans and a long black sweater. It wasn't fancy, but that was one thing I did like about coming home. Things were much lower key in Salishan. In Seattle, I always felt pressure to have the right shoes, the right gloss, the right purse. Odessa was great at that kind of stuff; I always felt a little awkward in anything but work out gear.

"As long as there is a beer with my name on it I'm good," I said.

"Fucking crazy about Troy, am I right?" Max asked. "Like the past is smack, in your face."

"Max, don't tease Shea," Caiden said, his voice steely.

"He broke her heart, remember?"

"I'm fine," I said, looking at the window. I was afraid if I made eye contact with either of my brothers they'd see right through me.

We pulled into the Gold Digger parking lot.

Caiden parked and walked around to unlock out door.

"Thanks for giving us hardened criminals a ride," Max said. "Now let's go have some fun, when was the last time the O'Toole siblings went out and raised hell."

"Not raising hell tonight brother, "Caiden said.

"He has gotten so serious since joining the law," Max said.

I grinned and took a breath knowing it has been ten years since I'd walked into this restaurant and bar. Back in the day, the Gold Digger hadn't exactly been sticklers about ID. I'd joined plenty a party in the back rooms without even flashing a fake ID.

The three of us walked through the front door and down a hall with swinging doors like an old-time saloon. I stood in the center of the sawdust floor. Music pumping, the tables were filling up but not overcrowded. At a glance, I had already spotted two girls from high school and an old girlfriend of Max's named Roxanne. Apparently so did he.

"I'll join you both in a minute," Max said, nodding at

Roxie and turning on a megawatt smile that I had to admit looked pretty fine. "Hello gorgeous," he said, his voice booming as he crossed the floor.

"Does he ever get tired of trying to get laid?" I asked Caiden.

Caiden put his arm around my shoulder. "It's how he copes with stress."

Max slid into the booth beside Roxie, his arm already around her shoulder. They looked like they were about a pint away from leaving together.

Caiden led me to a slightly quieter table in the back of the room. "Plus he's worried about Dad. We all are."

"If we are so worried," I said, sliding into the booth, "why are we out drinking?"

"Because Max is right. If we all sat around watching Dad he'd probably die just to piss us off."

I put my head in my hands. "So, we are out drinking."

"So, Dad will survive."

"You two are crazy."

Caiden smiled. "He is. I'm just his brother."

We looked over to see Roxie and Max, lip locked. "Damn he works fast," I said.

"What can I say he's a good looking guy," Caiden said, grinning and running his fingers through his blonde hair.

"You know you could have your pick of the women in this town," I said.

"I don't want the pick of the town," he said, signaling one of the servers.

"You could look up Megan," I said, bringing up Caiden's college girlfriend. They had been really serious until something terrible went down. Caiden was pretty tight lipped about what had happened, but I knew he hadn't really been serious with anyone since.

"And I don't want to talk about it," he said, as our waitress approached. "Hello, Celia. Shea you remember Celia. She was a year behind you."

"Evening," she said. "Nice to see you out and about Officer O'Toole."

Celia was short and curvy with the longest eyelashes I'd ever seen. "I'll bring you all a pitcher," she said. "How many glasses you need?"

"Three," I said. "Paul Ingram's coming."

Celia's eyes widened and her cheeks flushed. "All right then, I'll be back with your pitcher and with Paul's," she said, stammering. "His usual I mean. I know what it is. I have it memorized," she wrinkled her nose and pointed to her head. "In my brain."

She was adorable and kept talking as if she had no off

switch. "I memorize a lot of things about Paul," she said. "And other people, I mean. Okay bye for now." She scurried off in a flurry.

"Wow," Caiden said. "Somebody is head over heels . . ."

Seeing how Celia got so carried away by her emotions, made me think of how I'd behaved that morning in the orchard.

"I kissed Troy this morning," I blurted, just as the music changed up to a song about no good lying lovers. Odessa was right. My life was a bad country music song.

"Excuse me?" Caiden said, reaching for his non-existent beer. "When I found out Troy was back, I figured you were either going to hit him or sleep with him and since you slapped him yesterday, I figured you'd made your choice."

"I feel like such an idiot," I said, covering my eyes. "Troy came to the orchard. He intercepted me in the back valley."

Celia reappeared holding a tray with glasses and a pitcher. "Here you go," she said. "I'll bring another pitcher when Paul gets here too." She spun around on her heels and made a beeline for the kitchen.

"The orchard. Isn't that where you two used too . . .?"

Caiden said, his eyebrows dancing.

"Ew . . ." I said. "I do not want my big brother remembering things like that."

"I'm not remembering it like I am reliving it Shea," Caiden said. "It's just you two weren't as discrete or as sneaky as you think."

"Whatever, yes. He found me back there and it was like I couldn't resist him. I was super mad and there was no way I was going to touch him but then he moved so close." I took a breath remembering the energy between us. "All of a sudden I was eighteen again and then he kissed me." I rolled my eyes and took a big sip of beer. The ice cold liquid rolled down my throat. It felt good hitting my empty stomach. I was going to need to watch myself if I intended to stay anywhere close to sober.

"You two had a connection that summer," Caiden said. "He broke your heart."

"A connection? I wanted to marry him Caiden," I said, eyes wide. It had been so long since I'd admitted those words out loud. "I was only eighteen and I said yes. We were so in love. I mean it's crazy, right? I wrote that letter to Mom and Dad and told them I was running off. Troy must have figured out it was nuts, right? That's why he left me that day."

"I don't know if you'll ever be able to answer that."

"I mean, who does that? Who leaves an eighteen-year-old girl on the courthouse steps?"

Caiden shrugged and sipped his beer. "A scared eighteen-year-old boy?"

"You with your sense of justice and empathy," I said, already feeling a bit warm from the alcohol. "I feel a little bad about slapping him. I'm sorry Ben punched him too. Look at you with your delinquent family. Where is Ben tonight anyway?"

"Not sure," Caiden shrugged.

"But you know everything about everybody in this town. You're the law."

"I enforce the law. I try not to get into people's business."

I looked up to see Paul making his way through the now crowded room. His cheeks flushed he looked a little lit up already as he slid into the booth next to me. "Hey O'Toole clan," Paul said. "What brings you two out to a dive like this?"

I laughed. "Your invite idiot."

Caiden just nodded and raised his glass. Max was on his feet slow dancing with Roxie to a fast song. His hands on her lower back, his body pressed against hers. I figured he was most definitely getting lucky tonight if not in the next few hours, before sunrise at the very least.

Paul leaned across the table. I got a whiff of heavy cologne that made me gag a bit. It was a musky cinnamon blast that reminded me how Paul tended to overdo things a bit.

"You want to dance Shea Marie?" he asked.

"Sure, why not?" One beer coursing through my veins and I thought dancing was a good idea.

Paul took both my hands and led me across the floor. His grip was strong and confident. He spun me in a circle and then away from his body like a yoyo. He may have smelled like an accident at a cologne factory but the man knew how to swing. I couldn't help but giggle. "You still swing dance like when we were younger," I shouted over the music, laughing as he made me dizzy, spinning me back and forth like a boss.

"Heck yeah," he said. "You were always the best dance partner, though."

"Remember all those dances we went to, together?" I said, laughing. It felt so good to travel down memory lane with an old friend. "How many did we go to?"

"Five," he said. "I have a good memory."

"Hey you should think about dancing with . . ." I was

63

about to say Celia when I saw Paul's face cloud over.

"What is it?" I asked.

Then I felt a tap on my shoulder. Troy stood on the dance floor looking like a man at the wrong party in his three-piece suit.

"May I cut in?"

"No," Paul said, turning me away from Troy before I could answer. I hadn't intended to say yes, but the gesture pissed me off.

"I got this," I said.

"Shea, you don't need that guy."

"I think you should let her decide for herself," Troy said, taking a step forward.

"I think you should back out of this place and go back to wherever you came from," Paul said, pushing out his chest.

The two of them looked like two roosters facing off before a cock fight.

"Oh for Christ sake. Cut it out, both of you," I said. I waved to Caiden who got out of the booth slowly as if he needed to save his strength.

Troy and Paul still faced each other both of them looking prone and ready for a fight.

I stepped between them my hand on their chests. "Paul,

sit down," I said. "And Troy knock it off. You two are being ridiculous.'"

"I need to talk to you," Troy said to me.

"You don't get to come in here and tell me what to do," I said.

"I need fifteen minutes."

In a sea of plaid shirts and denims, Troy stuck out like a sore thumb in that ridiculously beautiful suit. And when I looked into his eyes once again I saw the boy I loved before. Damn him and his dimple.

"Don't waste your time with him," Paul said, grabbing my hand.

"Hey," I pulled away from him. "I can make up my own mind, thank you very much."

"Yeah, she can make up her own mind," Troy said.

"Don't get cocky," I said to him. "You've got fifteen minutes. Talk."

"Not here," Troy said, taking my hand he led me across the dance floor. I looked over my shoulder at my brothers and Paul who stood shoulder to shoulder like an offensive line. I knew with one word I could unleash a whole lot of drama in the Gold Digger that night and most of it would end up with a fist in Troy's face.

I was angry, but I didn't want to hurt him.

I was just grateful that Ben was nowhere to be found. He wouldn't have backed off even if I begged him.

"I'm fine. I'll be back," I said.

I waved off my brothers and let Troy lead me out of that sawdust room. It felt familiar, this feeling of escape. My hand clasped Troy's as we ran into the dark many times before, but that was the past, not the present. So why did every step I took feel as though we were traveling together back in time.

CHAPTER 6

I shook off Troy's hand as soon as we stepped into the parking lot.

"Talk," I said, arms crossed and taking a step onto the covered porch by the front door.

He gave me a crooked smile and brushed back his dark hair. "We can't talk here, Shea."

"Sure we can." I shrugged as a couple that looked vaguely familiar to me headed towards the front door. "Hey," I said, nodding at them and stepping out of their way.

"Shea, come on," Troy said. "This is the most popular place to drink on a Saturday night. We stay here not only are we going to get interrupted every two minutes, but everyone in town is going to be talking about us . . ."

"Fine," I sighed, brushing back my hair. One thing I hated more than gossip was being in gossip's crosshairs and Troy was right. Salishan was a small town and most people knew our history, seeing us together would cause some buzz. "You got a car?"

"A car and a destination."

"I said fifteen minutes," I said.

"I know and I'm hoping you'll give me a few minutes

more." Troy looked vulnerable standing beneath a streetlight in that dirt parking lot. He was so out of place this side of Salishan. This was where the real people lived, the people who stayed in Salishan year round. People here worked the land. They knew how to read the weather and predict how much snow would fall based on how the clouds gathered along the mountain range.

Troy belonged on the other side of town, where big houses lined the lakeside. He was right that this was the busiest bar this side of Salishan, but even back in the day there had been chic little wine bars cropping up on the other side of town.

"Please?" He asked, looking up at me shyly. "You won't regret it."

It was a little hard to breathe standing so close to him.

Our eyes met and I was aware of my heart beating against my chest. I felt the pulse of blood rushing through my veins. Standing close to this boy who was now a man, I felt my core temperature inching upward strong and steady.

"I'll go with you," I said slowly, afraid that my judgment was clouded. "But if I decide at any moment I want to go home, you will give me no shit."

"No shit," he repeated.

His Three Piece Suit

"You will turn your car around and bring me straight back here or home or wherever I want to go and you will never bother me again and I mean never." I slowed my voice even more and stared him down. I hated to admit it to myself but saying these words pained me. Then I remembered that I'd cut this man out of my life once before, I would do it again. He no longer deserved a place in my heart. Whether or not he still had one wasn't the question. He didn't belong there. If I was going to trust him tonight, he needed to know that the stakes were high.

I didn't need to survey the overprotective male posse in the bar behind me to know that they wouldn't approve of my decisions so far, but I had to admit a part of me was more than a little curious to see what Troy would do next.

"If that is what you want," he said. "I accept your conditions."

"Fine," I said, arms crossed. "I'm in."

His face broke out in a wide smile and I swear his shoulders sagged with relief. "All right then, let's go before you change your mind." He clicked his key ring and the lights flashed and beeped on a sporty black car in the lot. It was the only vehicle within eyesight that wouldn't qualify as a rig or a truck and it wasn't covered in dirt.

"That's your car," I said, stopping. "The one you were

driving yesterday was silver."

Troy sighed. "That's my other car. Which I suppose you're going to give me shit for."

"Nah," I said, walking to the shiny black vehicle that clearly cost more than all of the cars in my dad's fleet of trucks combined. "I'm not going to give you shit."

"You're not?" he said, looking confused.

"I can't blame you for staying true to your roots," I said, opening the door. "You're a suit Troy. Always have been. Always will be."

I didn't wait to see the look on his face as I climbed into his car. I was a little ashamed at myself, like I'd just punched him below the belt. It was juvenile and it made me feel like a mean girl, but I was angry at Troy and his expensive clothes and fancy car.

He'd come into Salishan ten years ago the same way and managed to make me believe he was something more than summer money. He'd made me believe we were cut from the same cloth when clearly he'd been putting on a show.

Without a word, Troy sat down in the driver's seat and started the engine. He pulled out of his parking place and headed toward the street.

I glanced over my shoulder in time to see my brothers,

including Ben, and Paul standing on the porch outside the front door. They pointed to the car as we pulled out into the main drag a little too fast.

Oh well, so much for escaping under the radar. My poor choices were sure to be the subject of conversation at the barroom table. I only hoped the boys were smart enough to keep the fight to themselves this time. I was glad Troy had suggested we leave.

Troy drove us through the streets of Salishan away from the center of town.

"Where we going?" I asked.

"Somewhere we can both breathe," Troy said, and smiled. Passing beneath a streetlight, I could see tiny laugh lines etched around his eyes. Even so, I could see him as a boy sitting beside me in his Uncle's car and promising me the world. I remembered the way he'd reach across the seat and hold my hand while he drove.

The boy I once loved was driving me into the night.

The boy who I once loved had broken my heart, I reminded myself.

Still as every second passed, my heartbreak felt a little weaker while the memory of Troy's touch grew stronger.

* * * *

We drove through town towards Salishan lake and the

winding road that wove past the summer houses. Troy pulled down a dirt road at the very edge of Dad's orchards and left the car idling.

"You okay if we head down here?" He asked.

"Again?" I looked down the road ahead of us. Headlights illuminated the dark and revealed rows of apple trees to our left and right. I knew where he was leading me. This was the back road he had used to intercept me on my morning run. This was the path to the place where we'd met what seemed like a thousand times that summer.

This was where we had fallen in love.

This was where I had given myself to him body and soul.

And I needed him to know it meant nothing to me anymore.

"Sure, whatever," I shrugged. "Any place is fine with me." I held his gaze for a moment almost daring him to challenge me. I wanted him to know how little this place mattered. I only hoped he hadn't noticed my shaking hands.

"All right then," he said, and continued down the road.

I concentrated on looking out the window. My fingertips fiddled with the door handle I focused on the shadows of apple trees that stretched for miles up the hillside. The road was bumpy and uneven. Troy's little sports car bounced around a lot more than one of my father's trucks. I worried a little that we'd get stuck in the mud running so low to the ground.

"So, how's your Dad feeling?" Troy asked, as the car bumped and lurched heading closer to the valley.

"Ornery," I said.

"I am going to take that as a sign he is feeling better." Finally, the ground leveled out. Troy pulled the car over between a few trees and turned off the engine. "Can we sit outside and talk?"

"You want to sit out there?" I said, pointing to the grass.

"I have wanted to sit beside you and talk under the light of these stars for ten years, please Shea."

My stomach clenched. The emotion in his voice was thick with something that sounded like sadness. I wasn't sure if I was imagining things but I thought I saw the glint of tears in his blue eyes.

"Fine. It doesn't matter to me either way," I said, keeping my voice strong. I got out of the car and with my back turned took a deep breath shaking my hands in the air.

I needed to stay calm.

This place meant nothing to me.

I was just talking to Troy like we'd talked so many

times before.

I turned around to see him laying a blanket out on the grass.

"Oh come on," I snapped, my voice rising.

"What?" He looked up at me his eyes wide.

"No way!" I shouted at him and just like that I was no longer cool and collected. My pulse roared in my ears and my body shook with emotion.

"You said you were fine talking here," he jumped to his feet.

"And you were dumb enough to believe me," I said, my breathing hot and full of tears I could no longer hold back. Goddamn. I had officially lost control.

"I'm sorry, I've been thinking about this for so long," he said, running his hands through his thick dark hair. "What I would say to you, the way I wanted it to be, I've thought about it so many times. I didn't want the business with your family to come between us. I just thought if we could be together, the way we were before." He reached for my hand and I slapped it away.

"Don't," I said.

"Shea, I was a boy, a foolish boy. I'm not a boy anymore."

Troy stood in front of me. The blanket was spread on

the grass right behind him. Stars glittered overhead. The air felt cool but not cold. It was the perfect temperature for being together outside. The heat of our bodies would feel just right in that sweet evening air.

What was wrong with me?

"I should never have left with you," I said, crossing my arms.

"And I never should have left that day," he said. His fingertips reached out and grazed the back of my hand. I stepped back and he held up his hands. "I'm sorry. I will give you your space. If you want me to take you back, you say the word and we will leave this place."

I looked up at him standing in the moonlight. The white of his shirt gleamed in the dark. In that moment, he looked gorgeous and sorrowful exactly the way I had always wanted him to be.

"You never even said good-bye," I said. Saying the last word out loud took effort. "How could you do that to me?"

"I didn't think you wanted me to," he said. "But, I know now it was a mistake to walk away without a fight. I'm so sorry for hurting you, for giving up on us so easily but things were so far gone, I didn't see a way back to us."

A way back to us.

Hearing those words from Troy made me dizzy, as if the world were spinning just a little too fast.

"I was just a boy," he said, still giving me my space. "I didn't know what to do."

I stood perfectly still, my breathing shallow, my legs unsteady as the world spun faster and faster. Troy was so close and I ached to feel my arms around him. My body yearned to feel the heat of his body next to mine.

"Please forgive me," he said.

In a rush, I stepped forward and pulled him towards me and pressed my lips against his.

I collapsed into his kiss. Ten years of heartbreak slipped out of me and poured to the ground as my lips touched his.

This was the way back to us, through this kiss.

I leaned into his body as years of grief and sadness dissolved at our feet.

"You feel like home," he gasped. Our kisses grew more frantic. His lips moved down my neck to my collarbone. His hands slipped beneath my sweater.

I rocked back as he ran his hands up and down my skin and over my breasts. I inhaled as my nipples hardened and a shock wave of pleasure moved through my body.

"Take me," I whispered. His eyes never left mine as I

walked backwards carefully stepping until I felt the blanket beneath my feet. I kicked off my shoes and dropped his hand so I could unbutton my jeans.

Troy watched me undress until I stood in the moonlight in my bra and panties. I wasn't even cold in the night air.

"You are more beautiful than I remember," he whispered.

"No more talking," I said, I stepped forward and grabbed his tie, tugged him towards me, and wrestled with the knot as we kissed. Then I moved onto the buttons of his shirt, they were so tiny and troublesome, he finally pulled his shirt open, buttons flying.

We both laughed between kisses as his suit jacket and pants dropped to the ground.

I felt this sense of joy that had been missing with my other lovers. This was the man I loved. He had come home to me. His body felt different, but I recognized his touch, his taste. I ached to feel him inside me. I wanted to know what kind of lover he had become in our years apart. I wondered if I would recognize the feeling of him sliding deep inside. Would we fit together like we had all those years ago?

Troy lifted me up and lowered me to the ground in my

panties and bra. His tongue ran down my neck as he undid my bra exposing my breasts in the moonlight.

He slipped out of his boxers and socks as I shimmied out of my panties.

Finally, we were totally naked together, lying beside each other on the blanket. His skin felt electric. I could not stop touching him as my hands ran up and down his muscular arms.

Then he hovered above me, his lips at the base of my throat, he kissed me softly moving over my breasts and taking my nipple into his mouth. His finger found my wetness as he gently sucked and teased me. My body tensed with pleasure. This was familiar and different in a sexy and delicious way.

My hand found his erection. I felt myself grow even wetter as I grasped his hardness and imagined him pushing inside of me, bringing me to climax.

We made out like crazed teenagers. I stroked his dick until I felt a bead of cum forming at his tip. Then Troy's breathing slowed and he gently removed my hand.

Without a word he hovered above me again, his body glimmered with sweat. Then he kissed a line down my body but this time he didn't stop at my breasts he continued until he was between my legs.

His Three Piece Suit

He parted my lips with his fingertips and kissed me tenderly at first and then with an increased pressure.

My legs propped up on his shoulders he buried his face in my pussy rocking me harder and faster.

I moaned and leaned back, feeling dizzy with pleasure and need. With my hands in his hair and my inhibitions totally gone, I pressed Toy's face against me harder. I arched my back and moved against his lips and tongue, moaning.

My body tensed until an orgasm rocked through me. I leaned back quivering.

"I want to make you come every day," Troy whispered, his lips against mine.

I lay beside him, my body rippling still with heat and pleasure.

"Make love to me," I whispered.

"You sure?" he asked

"I've never been more sure," I said.

He nodded and I heard the sound of him unwrapping a condom. For a second, I wondered if he'd brought it hoping he'd get lucky. It didn't matter. I didn't feel as though this was Troy getting what he wanted, this was me taking what I needed. This was me finally letting go of my anger and pain and allowing my heart to open up again. Where it would lead, I didn't know. I only knew that I wanted this now.

I spread my legs and moaned at the feeling of his hard cock pressed between my legs.

"I've dreamed of you for ten years," he whispered, his cock teasing me. I swear he could have made me come with a single brush against my clit. I placed my hands on his lower back and pulled him toward me.

I gasped at the sensation as he pushed inside me. With each thrust all the memories of making love to him that summer came rushing back one by one.

He pushed in deeper.

I remembered the first time we kissed.

The first time we'd stood naked before each other, so vulnerable and so in love.

We made love on that blanket that night as if no time had passed.

We made love on that blanket as if our bodies were made for each other.

We made love until we couldn't hold the pleasure back anymore.

The spark of heat between us grew until it was a roaring fire.

"Now. Now. Now," I gasped, rocking and moaning I

came in a rippling wave. Troy followed shuddering above me his body pressing into mine.

We lay perfectly still side by side, the only sound was our breathing and the distant sound of crickets in the night.

The flashlight hit me right in the eye before I ever heard the rustle of footsteps.

"Jesus Christ!" A voice boomed in the darkness.

"That's Ben," I gasped. I rolled away from Troy and scrambled for my clothes. I looked up in time to see the flashlight moving towards us quickly.

"You mother fucking son of a bitch," Ben said, rolling up his sleeves and striding across the grass.

"Not again, come on," I shouted, back on my feet and zipping up my jeans.

Troy jumped to his feet naked and reached for his clothes. "I don't want to fight you, bro," he said backing away.

"Sure you do," Ben said, his voice heavy with alcohol. I pulled my sweater over my head and jumped in between them. Footsteps pounded on the grass behind us as Caiden, Paul, and Max came running.

"Caiden, Max . . . stop him," I pleaded, blocking Troy as he pulled on his clothes. "What's wrong with you!" I screamed at Ben. "Get the hell out of here."

Ben ignored me lunging for Troy but Caiden and Max had him by both arms before he got in another swing. Together with Paul's help they dragged my brother off the blanket. He fought against them like a wild and angry bull.

"Come on Ben," Caiden said, his voice low and reasonable. "Let's just walk away man, walk away."

"He is the one who never should have come back," Ben said, struggling to break free. "He's a fucking liar, Shea. And he's using you."

"I need you to stop punching people, Ben," I shouted at him. My clothes were on but I still felt totally naked. "Get him out of here, please."

"Sorry, Shea," Paul said. "Ben insisted we find you."

"Just get him out of here," I said, crossing my arms. I felt humiliated and blamed myself for allowing something so private to be exposed. Ben had seen me leave with Troy, I should have known he would do something stupid.

The boys dragged my drunken brother up the hillside, Paul followed a few steps behind. "Sleeping with the enemy," Ben shouted from the top of the hill. "Don't believe his bullshit. He's using you to get to our land. You're sleeping with the fucking enemy Shea."

"That's enough man . . . enough . . ." I heard Caiden's muffled voice talking him down but the words had stung.

82

His Three Piece Suit

Was Ben telling the truth? Was Troy being honest with me, or was this seduction in the orchard all part of an elaborate plan to get back in my good graces? Was he truly remorseful, or was my heart just searching for a way to mend?

"Tell me what you want to do right now, and I'll do it," Troy said, softly.

"Home," I said, turning to look at him. "Please take me home.

Ben's shouts faded in the distance as Troy and I stood side by side in the dark. I hated how Ben's accusations wormed into my mind so quickly. That tender peace I'd felt in Troy's arms disappeared, replaced by infectious doubt.

* * * *

Making love to Troy had felt like a dream. My brothers finding us and threatening to fight him had felt like a scene from a bad made for TV movie.

I thought of Odessa and how she would laugh about my life in Salishan. This was just more evidence that life over here played out like a bad country song but suddenly the old joke didn't feel so funny to me anymore.

"Ask me anything?" Troy said, as we got into his car. He backed up, wheels spinning and for a terrible moment I was afraid we were stuck. I think Troy had the same fear as he grinned nervously and moved the car back and forth looking for solid ground.

"Please tell me we don't have to call my brothers for a tow," I said, massaging my temple. "That would be the worst."

"We don't," he said, "I got this." Then the car lurched forward and back.

I breathed a sigh of relief as we worked our way up the hillside.

"I don't have questions for you," I said. "Not right now."

"Ask me about the land," he said.

"No, I don't want to."

Troy turned to look at me. "You're afraid."

I said nothing and bit my lip.

"You're afraid that he's right, that I'm using you."

"You haven't used me." And just like that the walls were back up. "I'm a grown woman. I made a choice to have sex with you. I have that right. It was just sex Troy."

It had been a lot more than sex, but I could no longer admit that to him.

"I see," he said, eyes fixed on the road. We weren't far from the house. He turned down the drive, the lights were on upstairs and in the kitchen. I imagined I'd find Ben at the counter drinking black coffee, water, or passed out on the couch. He really needed to move out.

I hoped Caiden and Max were still awake. They each had their own place in town but I hoped they'd had the good sense to keep an eye on their drunken older brother.

I also felt guilty thinking about Dad at the hospital with Mom by his side. I was supposed to be home to focus on my family and I'd managed to do nothing but make poor choices with a man I wasn't sure I could trust.

"I think this was a mistake," I said, as Troy pulled the car to a stop in front of the farmhouse.

"That's your brother talking," he said.

"No, it's me. You don't have a dad in the hospital right now and a brother who has clearly lost his shit. He is under a lot of pressure and I don't think you are helping him in any way."

"About Ben," Troy said. "Ask him about the loans."

"Loans."

"Just ask," Troy said, his face pained. "I can sense that you are leaving me again and I can't take that. I can't lose you twice. I'm going to fight for you this time."

I opened the car door. "I can't believe you'd be so arrogant to think you had me back already. Good night." I slammed the door shut and on shaking legs walked to the farmhouse.

Ask Ben.

Ask Ben about the loans.

Son of a bitch.

What had my brother done?

CHAPTER 7

The house was totally quiet as I walked into Mom's kitchen. She had been away for days, but her blue and white gingham towels were folded by the sink. A series of embarrassingly awkward grade school photos sat in her greenhouse window behind the sink. Mom had given up on growing plants long ago although she kept the window boxes that framed the farmhouse windows blooming.

I picked up a photo of me with the boys, standing on the front porch. Max and Caiden looked like they were rough housing, arms wrapped around each other's necks. I never tired of seeing photos of them side by side. Nature's perfect copy they loved to call themselves.

Ben stood behind me in the photo, his infectious smile just starting to creep across his face. He was so lighthearted back then, so full of humor and energy. Where had that happy boy disappeared to, I wondered? He was so handsome and looked so much like my father. I wondered if the boy in that photo knew how much the responsibility of the orchard would weigh on him in the years to come.

And then there was me. Shea Marie.

Age seventeen I thought. It was funny how the years ran away from me.

There I stood, sandwiched between my brothers. I worshipped them all and wanted to be like them. I think that was one of the reasons I had jumped into cross-country and other sports. I wasn't a boy, but damn if I wasn't going to be just as strong as them.

What had that seventeen-year-old girl been thinking about that day? Did she know that she would soon meet a boy named Troy who would change her world? What would I have done if I'd known that the next year would bring me more heartache than I'd ever imagined.

I ran my fingers across that girl's face and wondered what she would choose if she'd been given the chance to change her fate.

What would any of us choose given the chance?

Ask Ben about the loans.

I inhaled as a cold feeling filled my belly.

"Good looking crew," a voice behind me said.

I turned to see Paul standing in the doorway.

"Hey," I said, leaning against the sink. "Is Ben . . .?"

"Passed out cold, yeah." Paul smiled and ran a finger through his wavy red hair. "Your brothers asked me to stick around in case you got home."

"Look, I'm a little embarrassed."

"Hey don't be," he said. "You are a grown woman

Shea and I swear I didn't see anything. You are entitled to do what you want . . ." his voice trailed off.

"Or, do who I want," I said, emphasizing the word do. I looked up at Paul and suddenly we were laughing, deep belly roll laughs that reminded me of the way we'd been in high school. Paul and I had been in the same class for twelve years and were best friends for a majority of that time.

Paul was an only child so he spent a lot of time hiding out in the chaos of our house. We walked to school together. We were partners at the science fair every year. We'd even gotten so good at forging each other's handwriting that we took turns writing each other's book reports. Things changed when Troy came to town. I remember telling Paul about my feelings for the new boy including details about our secret signal, one, two, three. Paul never said anything out right but I knew he wasn't happy that I'd fallen in love.

Before Troy, we'd spent hours up late watching movies in the rec room, talking about the places we'd go when we left Salishan forever.

After Troy, I moved away. Paul never left.

"Well, I'm going to head out of here," Paul said, walking to the kitchen door.

"You want me to drive you?" I asked. "I don't mind?"

"Nah, I'll walk," he said. "Reminds me of the old days and as you know it only takes . . ."

"Seven minutes to get home if you aren't a lazy son of a bitch," I said.

"Exactly."

"Can I ask you something?" I said, following him to the back door. Stars glittered overhead against the blackened sky. "Is Ben okay?"

"I don't know," Paul said, stopping. "He drank a lot tonight. You know he and Daisy broke up last May, he's not doing that great."

"What about the orchard? Is there trouble there, does he ever talk about it?"

"Well, I've been helping your brother out a bit ever since your dad started slowing down, Shea."

"What do you mean slowing down . . ." My stomach twisted into knots. "Caiden said, his heart attack came out of the blue."

"The old man has been declining. Ben knows this orchard, but he gets a little overwhelmed. I help out where I can, but there are some things I don't have access to." His eyes met mine. "After all, I'm not family."

"Oh come on, Paul," I said. "You are practically family."

"You know what I mean and it's not the same," Paul said.

I nodded and pursed my lips. "Okay then, I'll let you go."

"What did Troy tell you tonight?" Paul said. "How did he get you to . . . never mind."

"To have sex with him?"

Paul shrugged. "I wasn't going to be so crass."

"It just happened Paul," I said. "We went through a lot together."

"He left you that summer," Paul said, his voice tense. "I'm not judging, but . . ."

"But you are."

"It's just hard for me to understand why you would let a guy like that touch you again."

"He was my first love Paul."

"And he left you at the courthouse Shea. I was the one who found you there. I'd never seen you look so sad. It broke my heart too."

I looked at him remembering how I'd felt when he'd pulled up in one of my dad's trucks.

Everybody's looking for you, he'd said. *You want a ride home?*

I'd climbed into the cab and sobbed as if the world was

ending. It kind of was actually. I'd left a note for Mom and Dad saying I'd run away. Things were never the same between Dad and me after that. He'd looked me straight in the eye when I'd walked in the door and said one thing. *I'm disappointed.*

I'd wanted to die, so instead, I did the next best thing. As soon as the ink was dry on graduation day, I packed up and left town for good. I'd thought I was running from my memories of Troy. I saw now that I'd run from my family as well.

"I know he hurt me, and I hurt everyone when I left. Tonight was a mistake," I said, rubbing my eyes. "It won't happen again."

"What did he say exactly about Ben?"

"He said, ask him about the loans? You know anything about that?"

"No," Paul said. "No, I don't. I think he's trying to work you Shea. You know he isn't like us. He's different, he always has been. He has different values."

"I know the drill. He's summer money. He's a suit and we're cowboys."

"You got it."

"Well it's time I remembered why I'm home anyway. I need to focus on Mom and Dad, and helping my family, at least until I need to head back home to Seattle."

"Good night then, I'll see you around."

I watched Paul walk down our drive until he cut right onto a trail that led through the orchards. It was funny I had two different paths. The paths I'd walked with Paul as a friend and the path where I'd walked with Troy as his lover. Both felt complicated right now.

Upstairs I walked past Ben's bedroom door, careful not to make a sound. I slipped into my old bedroom, peeled off my clothes and slipped beneath the flowered comforter that had kept me warm for years. Sleep came quickly and I was grateful that Troy stayed out of my dreams.

CHAPTER 8

The next morning, I got up early for a run and then decided to go into town for some baked goods. Carbs equaled comfort and the boys and I had eaten through Mom's backlog of cookies, scones, and pies.

I always enjoyed driving the big rigs, so I took one of Dad's trucks and headed into town stopping at Daisy's bakery *Sweet Treats*. Ben's on again and sadly off again girlfriend owned the place and made the best cinnamon rolls I'd ever tasted. They were thick, gooey, and swimming in creamy icing.

Mom would say she'd gained ten pounds just by looking at them. I didn't care whether or not they had good fats or bad fats in them, I wanted to bite into something delicious and close my eyes without worry for just a few minutes.

The bell rang as I opened the door.

"Hey there." Daisy stood behind the counter wearing a white apron, her dark hair pulled into a ponytail. She had dabs of flour on her cheeks. Her face brightened when she saw me.

"Shea, how are you holding up? I heard from a friend at the hospital that your dad has been a whole lot of trouble."

Daisy winked and placed her hands on her ample hips. Ben had always loved women with super sexy curves and Daisy was his ultimate woman.

"Dad's cranky and wants to go home, which I think is a good sign. Has Ben been keeping you up to date?" I asked, knowing I was digging.

"I'm afraid not," Daisy said, biting her lip. "We haven't been in touch lately and that makes me sad. I don't know what your brother would do if something happened to that man."

It was funny, I had never thought of Ben in that light. He never came across as really needing anyone, especially our dad.

Daisy seemed to read my mind. "He hides it you know," she said, leaning down and pulling a tray of rolls out of the glass case that faced the café tables. She took out two big white boxes and without asking sliced up cinnamon rolls and nestled them in between sheets of wax paper. "Ben acts tough, and he hides behind all that attitude."

I took a seat at one of the tables so I could watch Daisy work. "I'm sorry you two are having trouble."

"Benjamin O'Toole has been my one and only for a while," she said, sighing. "I think if we get really lucky someday, we may just be each other's one and only at the same time." She plopped the white box on the counter. "It's on the house. I'm sorry I just assumed you were here for the rolls, was I right?"

"You assumed right," I said, standing. "And I came in here with real money. Actual dollar bills."

Daisy laughed. "I'm sure you did, but I also know that you probably woke up early this morning. You look like you've already gone on a run, pounding out your problems, and here you are thinking about everyone else bringing them something sweet on a hard day. You need to take care of yourself first, Shea."

"Are you sure you aren't a therapist, or at least psychic?"

"No," Daisy said. "I'm just a baker. And I've grown up watching you O'Toole's." She grinned and then her smile faded. "How are you doing with . . . you know?" Daisy nodded out the window with a pained expression on her face.

She didn't even need to say his name.

"He's back," I said.

"I know."

"Well, I'm a disaster. I slapped him in the hospital, then kissed him in the orchard and then did a bit more." I leaned on the counter. "Did you hear that my brother's saw us last night . . . you know?" I opened my eyes really wide and tried to send her a look. "We were . . ." I let my voice trail off.

"Yikes," she said, grimacing for a moment and then smiling a dreamy smile. "Well, he is a fine looking man, he always has been. I've seen him a few times in town wearing that fancy suit. You know, I think he's gotten better with age."

"Yes, he has," I sighed, rubbing my eyes. "But Troy Van Rossum and I were doomed from the moment he arrived in Salishan. It just wasn't meant to be then or now."

"That's not true," Daisy said. "I remember when you two met."

"You do?"

"It was the night of that big orchard party. Ben bought Max and Caiden that keg and most of your class was there pretending they'd gotten an actual invitation. Then in walks this boy, wearing blue jeans so stiff you could snap them in two and that enormous cowboy hat."

I laughed. "He wanted to fit in."

"And then all he wanted was you," she said. "Ah, young love."

"Young love," I said. "You are not that much older than me Daisy and you and Ben . . ."

"We are fire and ice honey, on again off again," Daisy sighed. "I think our trouble started back when he dropped out of school and that was a long time ago."

"I'd forgotten about that," I said. I had a vague memory of Dad injuring his back and Ben coming home to help out.

"Yep he was at Central University studying architecture." Daisy said. "It was hard on him quitting and for years I tried to talk him into going back but he never thought there was room for his dreams in the orchard life."

"I always thought he wanted to run the orchard," I said.

"And I always thought he wanted me honey, but now look where we are," Daisy laughed. "I'm worried about him this time," she said, biting her lip.

"Do you think he's having any problems with the orchard?" I asked.

"I don't know," she said. "But he's been shutting me out for a while. It's what he does when he's stressed and not happy."

"Maybe it's an O'Toole trait," I said. "I've been a little stressed and unhappy and I've only been home two days. I lost my temper with Troy last night. You'd think slapping him in the hospital would have given me some sense of closure. Apparently it wasn't enough."

"Can I give you some unsolicited advice?"

"Um, if it's unsolicited aren't you going to give it anyway?"

Daisy looked perplexed. "Just call the man Shea."

"You don't think I'm sleeping with the enemy like Ben?"

"I told you to call him, not drop your panties, and no, I don't think he's the enemy. I do think that you should know more before you go any further . . . not because I think it's wrong for you to have sex with the man," she laughed, shaking her head. "Sometimes I think it's hard for me to realize you're a grown woman."

"Seriously, Daisy. I'm almost thirty."

"Yeah, but you were always Ben's little sister."

"And you were always his girlfriend."

"Well, I'm not his girlfriend now, but I know what love looks like and you two loved each other."

"And you remember how he left."

"I remember," she said, her voice soft. "And now he is back. The boy who pretended to be a cowboy has returned for his country girl."

"Are you going to break into song . . ."

"No . . ." she opened her mouth to say something, but then thought better of it. "Never mind."

"What?"

"No, it's the past, I shouldn't go poking around into things that aren't my business."

"Daisy please," I said. "Please poke."

"It's just, I always figured it was his family," she said, arms crossed. Her voice took on a conspiratorial tone.

"His family?"

"You know that aunt and uncle he lived with. They were summer people, here to vacation and stay on their side of the lake, not to hang with the locals. I always thought it was their influence that drove him away."

"Right," I sighed. "You make us sound like a regular old Romeo and Juliet."

"Oh, nobody's drinking poison, but you did leave for a while Shea. It's good to have you back."

"Thanks Daisy."

"Sorry." Daisy pushed the box of cinnamon rolls towards me. "I changed my mind. You do owe me one thing."

"Of course," I said, reaching for my wallet.

"No, not that," she said. "Don't be like me. Your brother and I are a perfect mix of foolish and stubborn. Each of us digging in and wasting time." Daisy reached out and grasped my hand giving it a squeeze. "Don't waste time with Troy, go find him. Find out why he really left that summer. You deserve to know the truth."

CHAPTER 9

I spent the day with Mom at the hospital, keeping her company while Dad slept. We shared most of the cinnamon rolls with the nursing staff, but saved a few for the boys. Caiden and Max stopped by but neither of them brought up the shit show in the orchard the night before. I couldn't tell if they were trying to be kind to me, or if they were tired of all the drama. I kept waiting for Ben to come charging through the door full of piss and vinegar, but he was a no-show that day. I figured it was just the calm before the storm.

That night, I climbed into my old bed and pulled the covers up to my chin. I kept thinking about Daisy and how unresolved things felt with Troy, but I couldn't bring myself to reach out to him, not yet. I was still worried about Ben and Dad, but for the first time in years I felt a real comfort in being home.

I had never realized how much energy it took avoiding all the people and places that reminded me of Troy including my own family. I'd been staying away for years trying to hide from my pain. Now that Troy was back in the flesh, hiding seemed like a waste of time.

I could stop lying to myself.

His Three Piece Suit

I wasn't over Troy.

I still wanted him and I was tired of pretending. I just wasn't sure what to do with the fact that the man still made me weak in the knees.

Closing my eyes, I took a breath remembering the heat of his mouth against mine, the brush of his lips at the base of my throat. He had loved me with such passion and hunger. It was fierce and raw unlike anything I'd ever felt before.

Troy said he regretted not fighting for me.

What did that really mean? How could he regret not fighting for me, when he was the one who walked away?

But did it really matter anymore, who had left who?

I thought of Daisy again and her plea to not make her same mistakes, to stop wasting time. Troy and I were both ten years older and hopefully ten years wiser. I knew that I felt a lifetime had passed since I'd been that brokenhearted girl standing on the courthouse steps in the dark.

What would have happened if we'd gotten married that day anyway?

I closed my eyes and tried to imagine Troy and I married for ten years. Would our passion still burn as hot and bright? Would we have children? Where would we have lived? Would my parents have ever forgiven me for running away?

A light flashed in my room.

One, two, three times.

I lay perfectly still my heart pounding. A long time ago this had been our signal, our secret sign.

One, two, three.

I climbed out of bed and pulled on my sweats with shaking hands. If I was wrong, I supposed no one would notice I'd left my room. And if I was right? My pulse raced and my stomach did a few somersaults in response.

Padding down the hall, I snuck past Ben's room, down the stairs and out onto the back porch. I stood outside for a moment breathing in the cold night air, telling my heart to slow and my breathing to steady.

"Troy?" I whispered, eyes straining to see him in the shadows. "Troy, I know you are out there . . ."

Troy stepped out of the darkness into a patch of moonlight by a lone apple tree. He wore blue jeans and a white t-shirt that looked blue in the moonlight. He held a hat in his hands.

I caught my breath. "You changed," I whispered, my eyes wide.

"You noticed," he said, walking closer, the glint in his eyes was wild and untamed. "I know you probably want your space, but I couldn't stay away," he said.

"I don't know what I want."

"I do. I want you."

As he got closer, I couldn't help but notice the way the t-shirt stretched across the muscles in his chest and over his biceps. His thick dark hair was rumpled and the way he held his head he looked more than a little bit like a young James Dean.

"There is one more thing," he said, clearing his throat. "Now if I were just a suit, could I pull this off?" He lifted up his hands and placed a cowboy hat on his head.

It was the same awkward black hat he'd worn on the night we met.

"You kept it," I whispered. I reached out and touched the brim of his hat pulling it down over his forehead. "It still doesn't fit you."

"I know but I couldn't bring myself to throw it away," Troy said. "About yesterday, I wanted to apologize."

"No more apologies," I said. "I mean it. Not about what is happening now, with the orchard or what happened between us in the past."

"No more apologies?" he asked studying my face for a moment.

"No more, we are done with that. Let's just *be* for a

little while and see how that goes," I glanced up at the house. "I for one would feel a lot more comfortable if we took a walk."

"All right then," he said, offering me his arm. Slipping my arm in his, we walked along the dirt path into the darkened orchard.

We crossed through rows of ripening Honeycrisp apples the air smelled fragrant and sweet. "You know being with you calms me," I said. "All day I've felt nervous and worried, wondering what to do and now that you are here I don't want to overthink everything anymore."

"I like hearing that," he said. "Not the part about you being worried and nervous, but the part about you wanting me close."

He reached over and held my hand, his fingers sliding between mine and locking into place as if they were made to be together. Heat rushed through my body as I remembered how much holding his hand had turned me on that summer. There had been times he had just held my hand and traced his fingertip up my arm and I'd be dripping wet yearning for him.

"We've wasted enough time all ready, don't you think?" I said.

He answered with a squeeze to my hand. His breathing

seemed to change as well and I was suddenly very aware of how close his body was to mine. I felt heat and electricity between us. His leg brushed against mine and I wanted him. He ran his thumb over the top of my hand and I imagined him naked above me. The tiniest touch between us felt electrically charged.

I stopped walking, my breath shaking with desire.

"Shea?" he asked, turning to face me. We stood in a patch of moonlight not far from one of the old apple packing barns. When I was a girl, these buildings had been used to keep the picked apples cold before being crated off for distribution. The refrigeration systems were shut down and the barns were sometimes used for storage. It had been a long time since I'd bothered to explore this part of the property. In front of us, the trail looped around the building and continued on down into the valley. Behind us, the farmhouse sat on the top of the hill like a beacon, the lights of the kitchen shining out like a pair of eyes.

"Come here," I whispered, taking both his hands in mine and pulling him towards the barn door.

He laughed as he stumbled forward, following me towards the building.

Still facing him, I let go of one of his hands and unlatched the door. I kicked it open with my foot and pulled him into the darkened room behind me. The air smelled musty and sweet. Moonlight streamed inside through a large set of windows that faced the valley.

"Kiss me," I whispered.

"You know I didn't come here just to take advantage of you in the orchard, again."

"Sure you did," I said.

"Next time you should come to my place. I'm back in the old house by the lake."

"I'm just waiting for an invitation," I said, giggling.

Troy's arm wrapped around my lower back and he pulled me towards him. The moment our lips touched we were wild and uninhibited. Making love to him on the blanket under the stars had felt like a dream, a sweet and sensual reminder of the past. Our bodies finding each other in the darkness of the barn was fueled by unbridled passion.

We stumbled backwards hands fumbling with each other's clothes. Troy pressed me up against the wall. I felt his hard cock pressing against me. It felt so sexy, so hot. I moaned softly unable to control myself.

I tugged on his leather belt sliding it out of his pants and dropping it to the concrete floor. His shirt and jeans followed so did my clothes. Naked we climbed on top of our clothes trying to avoid the cold concrete.

His Three Piece Suit

Troy sat down, his legs stretched out in front of him. He unwrapped a condom sheathing his cock and then I straddled him. I rose up, spreading my legs and guided him deep inside. He pushed up into me, his body hard and strong.

I slipped my hands over his as he held my hips and we moved together. I rose up and down, his shaft sliding in and out of me at just the right angle brushing up against that sensitive place inside me.

I moaned and leaned forward the pressure against my clit felt exquisite. Troy's hands moved slightly and he gripped me harder, spreading my cheeks apart with just the right pressure as I rode him. That feeling of being stretched and strained added an extra level of sensation to my body that made it difficult not to come.

Harder and harder, I rocked against him. Then his fingers found my nipples and he gripped my tits, twisted them slightly. His hands slid up to my lower back and he raised himself up so our chests pressed together. He kissed me as I continued to ride him.

"Take me," he whispered his voice husky and deep. "Take everything."

Our breath moved in rhythm, our bodies rocked in time, I felt myself opening up more. With every thrust, energy and heat gathered in my pussy tightening and spooling up until I was so tense, so tight.

He pushed up again and I moaned as my body released and I orgasmed, spinning and falling. I shuddered and moaned against him as he came inside me thrusting and shaking.

We collapsed on the ground on our pile of clothes. Steam clung to the windows. Our breathing calmed as we lay together, his fingers traced circles against my skin.

"You have no idea how long I've wanted this with you."

"Oh, I don't know, maybe ten years," I said, my lips against his throat, tongue running up his neck. He tasted salty.

"I know you still have questions about why I am here," Troy said. "I want to explain things to you . . ."

I held a finger to his lips. "No. Not now."

"But we'll have to talk someday," Troy said. "Just like I know that someday you are going to tell me it's time for you to go back to Seattle."

"But not today."

"You have a life there Shea."

"I know. But right now I have you," I rolled over and stroked his cock and felt him grow hard again. Then I knelt down in front of him and took him in my mouth.

His Three Piece Suit

Troy's breath changed as I licked and sucked his throbbing cock. I wanted to feel him shake. Faster and faster I felt his body tensing until he touched my shoulder, holding me back ever so gently.

Then he moved away and sheathed himself before positioning himself above me and pushed himself deep inside. It was almost too much stimulation, but my body responded. I raised my hips off the ground, pushed against him, and met his touch.

Deeper and harder we moved, moaning and grasping each other. My orgasm came faster than expected, it surprised me as I unfurled all around him. A moment later Troy followed, he collapsed on top of me dripping in sweat.

We lay beside each other shaking.

"I don't think we knew how to do that ten years ago," I said, catching my breath.

"Just think what we could accomplish together with a little more practice."

"I am not sure my body can handle another round with you," I said, laughing. "You exhaust me in the best way. I think it's time you walk me home, cowboy."

"Yes, ma'am," Troy said. He rolled over, resting his head on one hand. He played with my hair with the other. "Will you promise to meet me again Shea?" he asked. "I don't want to play games anymore."

"Yes," I said. Then I reached up and I held his face with my hands. "I know you mean well and I will talk to my brother about the orchard. I'm listening. It's hard for me to hear, but I am listening to you."

"That's good," he said. "I'm not trying to tell you what—"

"What to do, I know."

"I care about this place, Shea. I care about you."

"I know," I said, and I leaned up and kissed him. I closed my eyes and I imagined that time had stopped that summer, that Troy and I were just kids in love with our lives ahead of us. I kissed him and tried to find that girl inside of me who still believed in happily ever after.

CHAPTER 10

I woke the next morning feeling as though I had a secret, a delicious, sexy secret. My body ached in all the best places. I felt stretched and strained, and throbbed in a way that made me want to close my eyes and play back the memory of Troy inside me, the way his hands gripped my hips, the way he explored me with such a sweet and assertive touch.

I sat at the kitchen counter with a bowl of cereal. I had felt this before, this yearning, this fluttering, this need. It had just been a long time, ten years to be exact. I stirred my spoon in slow circles as I stared out the window at the apple trees.

The house was so quiet, it reminded me of those mornings after the boys had gone to school and Ben had left for the orchard at sunrise.

I hadn't realized it at the time, but there was such a simple peace to those sleepy mornings. Mom puttering through the house making sure Dad and Ben hadn't forgotten their lunch and checking up on me to make sure I made it out the door in time for school.

I had wanted to grow up so fast and the summer it all happened I wished I hadn't grown up at all.

Ben walked into the kitchen and made a beeline for the

coffee pot. "Morning," he said, his eyes bloodshot, cheeks ruddy. He grabbed one of the oversized mugs and poured himself a cup of black coffee and drank it down as though it were water.

I don't think I could have gripped my spoon any tighter. I hadn't seen Ben since the run in with Troy in the orchard. That awful night already felt long gone even though it had been just two nights ago. I wondered what Ben would do if he'd known that I'd been with Troy again and this time I didn't intend to stop.

"So, how are you feeling?" I asked, treading lightly.

Ben looked bloated with dark circles under his eyes. "I'm good, just up too late," he said, leaning against the counter after pouring himself a second cup. His hand shook as he raised the mug to his lips. I wondered if he thought he was fooling anyone. I wondered if he was tired of trying. Dad may have deluded himself into thinking that Ben was doing all right, but the tremor in his hand told another story.

"You know you will give yourself an ulcer with all that black coffee," I said.

"Beats falling asleep at noon."

"You need to rest. You look stressed Ben, are you stressed?" Ben was only thirty-eight years old, and I swear he looked more like a peer of Dad's than my older brother.

"Oh, I suppose you want me to fix my diet, and avoid dairy and bread and everything good on this planet."

"No, I think you need sleep, water, and exercise . . ." I said.

"Forget it Shea, I'm not one of your needy Seattle clients."

"Needy," I said, my blood pressure rising. I don't know why I bothered with him.

"It means I don't need to pay someone to tell me how to live, what to eat and drink. I mean seriously. I'm an adult. You are one too in case you've forgotten."

And there it was, the dig. I inhaled unable to hide the cringe.

"I see," I said, breathing deeply and trying to channel some inner peace. I was used to my Dad's suspicions about my hoity-toity Seattle life, but to think that Ben had somehow morphed into an old cranky man when I wasn't looking terrified me. Plus, I needed to find the courage to ask questions and I knew enough about the unspoken rules in the O'Toole house to realize my line of inquiry would be unwelcome. Little sister had lost the right to question Ben when she'd left town and put down roots in the big city.

For some reason in that moment I thought about

Odessa. Take no shit and taking names in life, she had said. Damn straight. My brother was in trouble. I wasn't going to be afraid of his bite and let him chase me off.

"So, how are things at the orchard?" I asked, pouring myself another bowl of cereal.

"They are good," he said, wrinkling his nose.

"Profitable?" I asked, trying to sound neutral.

"We get by." His eyes narrowed.

"You think our production numbers are on track?"

"I think that it's been a long time since you've cared at all about what happens in the tress behind this house."

"Ben, come on," I said. "I'm just asking."

"No, you are prying Shea." His cheeks flushed a deep red and he slammed his coffee cup on the counter. "So you believe him is that it? You believe that lying son of a bitch over your own brother?"

"This isn't about Troy. I'm worried about you," I said.

"Bullshit," Ben shouted, sweat beading on his forehead. "You don't get to pretend you care. You come home only when you have to and now you are taking the word of a stranger and getting all up in my business."

"It's our family's business."

"No, it's not, it's mine!" Ben shouted. "This place succeeds or fails under my watch whether I like it or not. I don't get to leave when things get hard, don't you get it?" He paused for a moment, his chest shaking with every breath. "At least you had a choice. I never did."

"A choice? Ben, what are you talking . . ." I thought about what Daisy had said at the bakery the day before. "Is this about school?"

"Tell Mom that I'll be back by this afternoon when she brings Dad to visit."

"Ben what do you mean you never had a choice?" I called to his back.

"Forget it," Ben said, not even bothering to turn around. He paused at the front door, still not looking back. "And you better think long and hard about where your loyalties lie, Shea."

CHAPTER 11

Mom and Dad came home from the hospital that afternoon for a visit. Dad still hadn't been given the green light to come home permanently, but the doctor's thought a change of scene might do him some good.

Max and Caiden drove since Ben was working. He said he had appointments with a number of the apple distributors to re-negotiate contracts. "He shouldn't be at the negotiation table without me," Dad shouted as Max rolled him up the makeshift ramp he and Caiden had added to the back steps of the house. "Get me out of this goddamn machine, I can walk by myself."

"Dad, I have told you that you need to start slow. Climbing stairs, lots of walking, yelling at people . . ."

"I'm not yelling," Dad shouted.

Mom rolled her eyes and gestured for Max to bring Dad down the hall to the main floor guest room. She had this idea that he needed some time to acclimate to his new room.

Dad's eyes bugged out when Max took him past the stairs. "No sir," he said, gripping the arms and starting to stand. "Stop right there."

"Jesus, Dad," Max said, lurching forward as Dad

almost tumbled onto the hardwood.

I stood pressed up against the wall watching this scene play out. I figured there were enough players involved already and I needed Dad to be speaking to me if I was going to get any information out of him about the orchard finances. If Ben wouldn't tell me what was going on, I'd go to the source.

"I'm going upstairs to my room," Dad bellowed.

"Dad, you are not going upstairs," Max said, a vein pulsing in his forehead.

"William, listen to your son," Mom said, her voice low and soothing.

"He is not my doctor and just because he went to a fancy school, he thinks he knows everything."

"Come on Dad," I said. "You are not being fair."

"The doctors are trying to kill me," Dad said.

"That's it. He's impossible," Max said, raising his hands just as Caiden walked in, he walked out.

"Where are you going?" Caiden said.

"I'm out. You deal with him. Arrest him for all I care." Max slammed the kitchen door.

This was going better than expected.

Dad sat in his chair, gripping the armrest, his chest rising and falling with unspoken anger. Mom stood beside him her fingers on the bridge of her nose. Caiden raised a hand and knelt beside my father.

"Hey dad," he said. His voice was so kind, so even. It was no wonder my brother was in law enforcement, he had a gift for bringing sanity to the insane. The world needed more good cops like him.

"Hello son," Dad answered after a moment.

"I understand you're pretty pissed off."

"Damn right I am, everyone around here is acting like I'm sick. I just want to go upstairs to my room."

"All right, all right," Caiden said. "Max just wants to help you, Dad. Shea and Mom do too." Caiden nodded at me waving me closer. "And it will be much easier for everyone to take care of you, if you agree to stay downstairs."

"That's right Dad," I said, stepping forward.

"Aren't you going back to Seattle soon?" Dad asked, glaring at me.

"Not right away," I said, swallowing. "I'm not going anywhere, not today."

"If you think that's a good idea," Dad said, shrugging. I couldn't help but notice a flicker of a smile crossing his face. "All right then, get me into the sickly room. But I'm not going to stay there very long."

"That's fine," Mom said, eyes wide she mouthed the word thank you at Caiden and me. "We're heading to PT soon anyway and then back to the hospital."

Dad opened his mouth to protest.

"Not another word out of you William O'Toole, not another word." Mom wheeled Dad down the hall.

"Shouldn't you be heading back to work soon?" Caiden said. "Don't you have clients?

"Not today," I said. "I rebooked for the whole week. I can stay longer if you need me to."

"Thank you," Caiden said, snaking an arm around my waist. He leaned his head over resting it against mine. "Did you see the way Dad smiled when you said you weren't going back right away? I did."

"I did too."

"I gotta run." Caiden kissed the top of my head and left just as Mom came down the hall.

"You all right Mom?" I asked.

Mom shook her head as if my voice had snapped her out of a daydream. She looked up at me, the tension in her face melting into a smile. "Shea, baby, I'm fine. I'm just tired."

"Is Dad okay?

"He's getting better," she sighed. "Your Dad needs to

figure out how to be sick. He's not that good at it."

"That's because he doesn't' believe he's sick," I said, stretching.

She hooked her arm with mine. "You sure you are all right staying a few more days . . ."

We walked arm and arm into the kitchen.

"Business is good," I said. "I can afford to take some time off. I've built up a nice cash savings for emergencies just like this."

"That's my girl."

"Mom, I don't want you to think I'm prying but do you know how things are going financially with the orchard?"

"Well," Mom said. She fiddled with the gold key she wore on a chain around her neck. "I used to be more involved but over time I was so busy raising you kids . . ." her voice trailed off. "I am embarrassed to tell you Shea Marie, that I don't know . . . I should, I really should."

"Can I ask you something else?" I hesitated. "Do you trust Ben?"

I heard footsteps behind me as I finished the question. I turned around in time to see Ben standing right behind me. "Ben," I stammered.

"No, I want to hear this?" he said, arms crossed nostrils flaring. "What do you say, Mom?"

"Benjamin your sister . . ."

"My sister hasn't given a rat's ass about this property and now she suddenly cares."

"That's not fair," I said, my pulse racing, hot tears filling my eyes.

"Ask me Shea," he said.

"Is the orchard in trouble?" I said, my voice shaking.

"What kind of trouble?"

"For God's sake," Mom said.

"Financial trouble," I blurted. "Is the orchard financially vulnerable since Dad . . ."

"Since Dad has declined," Ben said, running a hand through his black hair. I could see glints of silver in the kitchen light. "This is what you need to know. I am in charge. And I will find a way to keep this orchard in this family for generations to come. Is that good enough for you?"

"All right then," I said, swallowing.

"All right," Ben said. "Don't ask me again." He stomped out of the kitchen his work boots pounding on the hardwood floor.

The tears came hot and fast as soon as Ben walked out the door. Mom leaned over and took me in her arms. "You are trying to help honey."

"I try and all I end up doing is making people angry," I hiccupped.

"No you are doing good," Mom said, smoothing my hair just like she had when I was a child. I heard the sound of my father's voice calling for her down the hall. "I need to tend to your father, you wait here. I'll be right back."

I couldn't sit still. I felt like running through the hills. The truth was I felt like running over the mountains and all the way back home to Seattle. I walked outside, cell phone in hand. I kept glancing at it, looking, waiting for something.

Waiting for Troy, I realized.

I wanted to believe that he was thinking about me the way I was thinking about him. I wanted to talk to him about Ben and the scene in the house that day.

I had told him that I would see him again, but I couldn't bring myself to make that call. I knew I was letting my insecurity run the show. After all I was a grown woman and if I wanted to call a man, I should just go ahead and do it. But I couldn't pull the trigger. I was a ball of nerves like a high school girl agonizing over talking to her crush. What would I say to him if he answered?

Hey I'm thinking about you.

Hey, I want you again.

His Three Piece Suit

Hey, do you mind if I climb into your bed tonight?

Each phrase seemed too brash, too bold.

We had agreed to forget the past, but me finding the courage to tell Troy I wanted him out right, was a bridge too far. Even worse, a part of me was still afraid.

Troy left you once, he will do it again, a little voice whispered. Ben's right to be distrustful. What makes you think Toy's telling you the truth? Ben says there is nothing to be worried about. You should trust your big brother after everything he's sacrificed for this family.

I wondered if Daisy was right about Ben. How much had it cost my brother to give up on his dream? Maybe more than any of us realized.

I needed to talk to Troy, if my family wouldn't give me answers, maybe he could help.

I closed my eyes and breathed, forcing my heart to calm. Why did I feel so nervous? Taking no shit and taking names. It sure didn't feel that way. Why was it so hard for me to work up the courage to speak up for myself with Troy and my brother?

The truth was I wanted to hide from all the stress and worry I felt at home. I wanted to feel Troy's skin next to mine and taste the salt of his skin. I wanted to fall asleep beside him and feel his strong arms around me like a shield.

I wanted to escape.

Standing in the driveway, I glanced back at the house. Mom wanted to stay and talk, but it was getting hard to breathe inside those four walls.

Troy had said he was staying at his family's old vacation place. I'd been there enough times. It had been years but I still knew the way.

There couldn't be any harm in driving by, right?

I grabbed my keys.

CHAPTER 12

The Van Rossum family had built a house on Lake Salishan the summer Troy and I met. To call it a house was an over simplification. It was more of a compound with a main house, guest cottage, and a boathouse. After Troy left, I drove by that gated drive every day for a week, hoping that I'd see a light on in the main house, praying he'd come home to explain everything away, but he never did.

The gate remained locked.

The curtains stayed drawn.

Until now.

I pulled over on the side of the road by the gate. Down the winding gravel drive, the main house sat at the top of a grassy hillside backing up to the lake. A grand brick building with big white columns a light was on in one of the upstairs bedrooms.

A lot of people in town thought the house was tacky and overdone. It was very different from most of the cabins that lined the lake. Troy's aunt and uncle had hired an architect and a custom builder from back east. This was supposed to be the family vacation home, but it was only occupied one summer, the summer Troy and I fell in love.

Seeing the house alive unlocked another bank of

memories.

Troy and I sneaking up the stairs after dark, our hands all over each other.

Troy and I sitting on the end of the dock, our toes in the water kicking up waves on those hot summer days.

We had spent hours together, talking, laughing, loving each other. He knew my eighteen-year-old-self better than anyone and right now I could think of no one else in the world I wanted to talk to.

My hands shook with nerves, but I sent him a text.

Can we talk?

He fired back an answer right away.

Anytime. Any place. Anywhere. Now?

I felt a rush of relief move through my body. I couldn't help but smile as I answered.

Yes, please. Your old house.

I'll pick you up.

No. I'll come to you.

My body buzzed with anticipation. I would talk to him about Ben. Troy would help me fix this. I just knew it. I closed my eyes figuring I'd wait a few minutes before heading down the drive. Even though he had ambushed me repeatedly at my parent's house, I still had my pride. I didn't want him knowing that I was parked right outside. It was a good plan, until I glanced out my window to see Troy's silver car pulling up right beside me.

He rolled down his window, grinning. "You are a very fast driver."

"You caught me," I said. "I had to get out of the house, sorry I should have told you I was here."

"You don't have to apologize to me, ever," he said, lowering his head so his dark hair fell forward. "I'm glad to see you."

I gripped the steering wheel feeling self-conscious and relieved all at once. "I was just looking at the house, remembering," I said. "It feels strange being back here after all these years."

"You feeling nostalgic?" he asked.

"Yes, for lots of different things," I said, thinking of his kiss, his caress, his body next to mine.

"Let's go inside where we can talk."

"Yes, let's talk," I said, feeling breathless. Our eyes met and for a moment we said nothing, just stared at each other.

"I'm going to talk to you so hard," he said, eyes narrowing as he gave me a very wicked smile.

"You are so bad," I said, giggling. Troy had always had the ability to make anything sound like a dirty word.

"I don't know what you are talking about," he said, teasing. "Follow me down the drive before your brother gives us a ticket for blocking traffic."

Troy pulled in front of me. A moment later the black metal gate slid open. I had that same otherworldly feeling that I'd had as a girl. The gate was a portal to another realm where people drank from crystal glasses at breakfast and listened to classical music while planning their next excursion to the Mediterranean or the Hamptons or wherever rich people spent time.

I had never thought my family was poor and I still didn't. We were rich in land while Troy's family was just rich, period. They had statues of greyhounds gracing their driveway and we had Mom's potted petunias. They had custom lampposts lighting their drive and we sometimes strung Christmas lights along the inside fence.

The Van Rossum property and house had fallen into some disrepair. I'd heard through Caiden that the family paid an older couple to act as caretakers and make sure the pipes didn't burst in the winter. Besides that, the house had sat vacant. The rolling grass that led to the house was unkempt and wild. The white picket fence that lined the property was missing stakes here and there.

I parked behind Troy in the circular drive.

His Three Piece Suit

"How is your family?" I asked, standing on the covered porch as Troy unlocked the front door.

"We aren't really speaking," he said.

"I'm sorry," I said.

He shrugged. "Mom and I have never been short on conflict. This time she wanted me to work at Barry's firm, Barry's her new husband," he explained. "But I chose a different path, after you?" He said, holding the door open.

"She didn't want you to come back here did she?" I asked, stepping inside the foyer. The smell was so familiar. I closed my eyes and inhaled immediately seeing the foyer as it had been that summer. Sunlight glittering on the overhead chandelier, a bouquet of fresh lavender gracing the entry way table and reflected in the mirrors that flanked either wall. Everything had polished and glittered in those days.

Troy flipped on the lights. Today the mirrors were covered with sheets and the scent of lavender was still there but buried under layers of dust.

"Let's just say that Mom wasn't thrilled about the idea," he said. We stood facing each other at the base of the main staircase. At the top of the stairs there was a large landing with a window box that faced the lake.

I remembered falling up those stairs with him giggling

and kissing and praying we could make it to his room without being caught.

Troy caught me looking. He stopped and smiled at me, eyebrows raised with mischief.

"We had some fun here," he said, nodding.

My cheeks burned. It had been more than fun. It had been hot, sweet, sexy, innocent, and playful. Everything had been new in those days. His hands running up and down my body, his lips finding mine and exploring me in ways I'd never imagined.

He was the first man to make me moan.

The first man to make me come.

"You remember that time we were up in my bedroom and Aunt Mayra came home early," he said, his voice lowering.

I smiled. "I about died. We'd strewn our clothes up the staircase, I think she almost tripped on my shoes."

"You hid under my bed while I told her that I'd been doing laundry."

"Do you think she believed you?"

"No, I don't," He laughed.

I swatted his arm. "You told me she believed you."

He laughed. "What was I supposed to tell you? You would have never set foot in this house again if you'd thought we'd been caught."

"No sir, you are right," I sighed remembering the sweet rush of sneaking away with Troy. It was addictive then and it was addictive now. I was well aware how much I loved re-creating that feeling of escape, that spark of keeping our precious love secret.

"Standing here with you," Troy said. "I feel eighteen again. I want to take your hand and pretend that nothing has kept us apart. I want to pretend we are still in love."

"Still in love . . ." I murmured, afraid of the word.

He was standing so close. The house silent outside of the sound of our breathing. Suddenly his arms were around my waist and he lifted me up in one fell swoop and carried me up the stairs. I couldn't stop kissing him as he walked down the hall and into his old bedroom. He kicked the door open with his foot.

It was as if time had stopped. There was his king sized bed in the center of the room. The linens were different but I recognized the simple black headboard and matching night stand. His closet door open, I saw a row of matching black suits instead of the button downs and polo shirts from high school.

His room had one of the best views in the house with a Juliette balcony that faced the water. The French doors were slightly open curtains fluttering. It was so quiet I could hear the sound of the lake lapping against the shore.

Troy laid me down on his bed.

"You didn't take the big bedroom," I said, nodding down the hall.

"No," he whispered. "This room belonged to us, it was the only place I wanted to be in this house."

Standing above me, Troy took off his suit jacket and unbuttoned his shirt. He slipped it off standing before me in his black pants. I sat up on the bed and wiggled out of my t-shirt, then I jumped up onto my feet standing just above him. He kissed my collar bone gently and softly.

His hands at my waist, he unbuttoned my jeans and slid them off my hips dropping them on the ground. I lay back down on the bed wearing only my bra and panties. Being back in Troy's old bedroom amplified all of my emotions. His every touch felt as though it reached deep into my core. My nerves hummed at a higher frequency. My senses were flooded with the sweetest desire.

Troy slipped off his pants and wearing his boxers he knelt down at my feet. He drew a slow circle around my ankle with his index finger and then traced a line up the inside of my thigh stopping at my crotch. Then he placed his palm against my pussy and pressed before he hooked his fingers into my panties and pulled them off.

I scooted up to pull him towards me but he smiled and gently pushed me back down.

"No, no," he said. "Not yet."

My body tensed with anticipation. Troy spread my legs and kissed the inside of my thigh nibbling softly as his palm pressed against me and then released.

I moaned as a wave of pleasure rippled between my legs.

Then he knelt between my legs and spread my lips apart, his tongue dancing across my clit. I whimpered as he nibbled my pussy, his tongue darted inside me just enough to make me feel weak.

Then I felt myself opening up as he slipped a finger deep inside, filling me up. First one finger, then two, I moaned and arched my back wanting more of him, needing more.

"Please," I whispered. "Don't stop."

"I'll never stop," he said, his mouth stayed between my legs, kissing and sucking followed by the thrust of his fingers. Back and forth he rocked me, each thrust timed with his lips and his tongue. My breathing changed as my body grew tense with desire.

"Don't, stop, don't stop, don't stop," I whimpered,

back arching, thighs tight, I felt myself spooling up until the pleasure spilled over. I reached down, my fingers in his hair, I pressed his mouth against me leaning into him as I came in waves gasping and writhing.

I opened my eyes feeling dreamy and drunk on sex.

Troy traced his finger over my breast sliding beneath my bra running his finger over my hardening nipple.

I could feel his hard cock pressed against me.

Still quivering I rolled over and straddled him.

"Your turn," I said. I wiggled his boxers off revealing his rock hard cock. He unwrapped a condom and sheathed himself.

Then I raised myself up and slid down, pushing him deep inside. He reached up with one hand to hold my breast as we moved together. My pussy moved up and down, his cock slid into me deep and hard. At some point the energy changed from the sweetness of making love into the uncontrolled. I wanted him. I needed him. I lifted myself off him and on all fours, raised my ass in the air. "Take me from behind," I whispered. "I want you deep."

I heard him moving behind me then felt his hands on my hips and then his dick tickling and teasing me and then sliding deep inside.

My neck arched up at the sensation. I was dripping wet.

Wet with sweat and need.

"Touch yourself," he gasped, holding still for a moment. "Touch yourself and come with me. Come with me."

I nodded and reached between my legs finding my clit. He leaned forward, his hand covering mine as he pulled out slightly and guided my hand in circles.

"Come for me baby," he murmured. "I want you to feel good, I want you to know how much I need you, how much I want you."

I moaned as I felt that energy building again, that glorious tightening, that gasping and tensing before the sweetest fall.

Then his hand moved away and he held my hips moving me back and forth, faster and faster. I responded moving with him, my nipples erect, my mouth open, gasping and moaning until the orgasm rocked me.

My body shook so hard I thought my legs might collapse as he leaned over me throbbing and pulsing as he came too. I felt his lips on my lower back, his tongue danced across my skin.

He slowly pulled out and turned me over for a soft, sweet kiss. Neither of us had the strength for more.

I savored this closeness, this feeling of peace. I

realized in that moment, at least for a little while, I had belonged to him and it had been enough. With our bodies, we had erased all the worry about the property, my brother, my father, and the past. We had made love and nothing had mattered but us.

"Wow," Troy said, speaking first.

"Yeah wow," I answered.

We lay on the bed both staring at the ceiling.

"That was . . ." I started, words failing me.

"Amazing. Miraculous. The best sex I've ever had," he said. He rolled over and traced his finger along my collarbone and down my body and circled my nipple.

"Oh come now, we had some good sex that summer and last night if I recall."

"Okay the best sex I've ever had since the last time I had sex with you," he said.

I grinned and shrugged. "I'll take that."

He continued to play with my breast. I knew I should be exhausted but as my breathing changed I wanted him again. I laughed and rolled away. "You are dangerous. I wanted to talk to you and look at me, all I can think about is sex."

"You say that like it's a bad thing."

I stood up and wrapped a blanket around my shoulders.

"You know I didn't come here just to make love to you," I said.

"Sure you did," he grinned, propping himself up on his elbows he parroted our conversation from the night before.

"Troy Van Rossum you are arrogant and . . ." I stumbled.

"And right."

"I came to make love to you and to talk," I said.

"What do you want to talk about," he said, pulling himself up on one elbow.

I took a deep breath before speaking. "Tell me what you know about my family," I said. "I am ready for your help."

∗ ∗ ∗ ∗

"To the office," Troy said. He handed me a robe from the back of his door while he pulled on a t-shirt and pair of sweats. I followed him down the hall to a room with a large wooden desk beside a window that faced the lake. There were tall bookshelves on either side of the window draped with blue dust covers.

Troy sat down behind the desk and powered on a laptop. "I told you my company invests in property." He slid his laptop between us so I could look over his shoulder. We were looking at a map of Salishan lake with plots of land dotting the lakeside. "They've been working on this deal for a few years. My job is to expedite things and make sure the project keeps moving forward."

"What project?" I asked.

"You see the red properties along the lake?" he said, running a finger over the screen. "That's the future site of Salishan Cabanas. It's a series of old world vacation homes, the type of thing that people rent for the summer, winter time too."

"But aren't those people's homes?" I said.

"Most people have sold already Shea."

"And my dad's land isn't even waterfront."

"It's not, but it's right across the road and it has views of the water. The soil content is perfect for growing grapes, so there are plans to set up a winery on-site. This property will make Salishan a vacation destination and bring a lot of money to the local community. I can get your dad a really good price for his land."

"But that's not Salishan," I said. "Nothing ever changes here. These people don't want to sell to you."

"Actually some of them do. It's progress Shea," Troy said. "Sometimes change is good.

My heart pounded and anger flared in my belly. "You didn't grow up here," I said, my tone biting.

"No, but I care about this place."

"If you did, you'd know that the people who live here don't want this in their community." I turned and walked down the hall pulling the robe tighter around my body.

"This is coming Shea," Troy said, following me to his bedroom. "Ardent has already acquired 90 percent of the land that it needs to start development. Let me show you what they are doing."

I looked at him as tears filled my eyes. "I have to go," I said, picking up my clothes and pulling on my panties.

"Shea, let me help your family negotiate, I can make sure your parents end up with enough money to buy land on the other side of the lake."

"My dad will never sell. They don't want property on the other side."

"Your dad is going to have to sell. The bank will force him."

The land. I'd grown up hearing stories about Great Grandpa O'Toole coming to eastern Washington from Dublin. He'd started with a single acre of apple trees. He made his mark and now my generation was going to lose it? What had Ben done?

"Ben says there is no trouble," I whispered.

"And you still believe him."

"No. No I don't, but it doesn't matter. It will kill my Dad to give up his home. I can't let this happen Troy. You have to understand this."

"Look," Troy said, placing his hands on my arms. "I have known for months that your land is in financial jeopardy. I have kept that information from my partners. They could fire me, they would fire me, but I have been trying to figure out how to get your family to let me help."

"You think it's helping to force them to sell?"

"If your dad makes a deal now, he has leverage. The firm doesn't know about the pending foreclosure."

"Foreclosure?" The word made my stomach turn.

"If your Dad waits the offer won't be nearly as strong and I don't know what kind of a return he will see."

"Troy, why did you come back here?" I gasped, pulling on my pants. "Did you come here to do business or did you come back here for me?"

I think the question stunned him for a moment. "When I saw the project in Salishan come across my desk it was like a door that had been locked inside my heart opened up," he said. "I told myself that I wouldn't look you up, and then I saw how the property lines fell and I know your family would be impacted so I got involved."

"You came here for the project first."

"No, I came here for you," Troy said, his face red and desperate. "I can feel you pulling away from me. Please don't shut me out."

"I can't do this. I'm sorry. I should never have come here."

"Your dad is going to lose control of the orchards," he said. "For God's sake Shea, talk to your family. Let me help your family negotiate. Trust me."

Trust.

I stood frozen, staring into the eyes of the boy I'd trusted all those years ago.

"I can't do this," I whispered. "It was a mistake to start this up again."

"Shea, no," he said.

"We're a long way away from trust, Troy and you know it."

"We agreed to let go of the past. We need to forgive ourselves, both of us."

"We were dumb to think we could just wipe the slate clean, just like we were dumb kids back then," I said, taking big gasping breaths. "I don't trust you Troy. I'm sorry. I don't."

He looked at me, his eyes glistening with tears.

"It's been ten years and in all that time, I didn't even

manage to get over you," I said, picking up my clothes. I felt like an idiot for getting naked with him again.

"Maybe you aren't supposed to get over me. Maybe I'm not supposed to get over you," he said, darting around the room, pulling on his clothes. Hands raised he was just a few feet away from me dancing between me and the door.

I took a breath and threw back my shoulders trying to fight my tears and failing. "Look, I think you want to help in fact I think you are trying to make things better. Part of me believes you, but this is no good."

"Shea, please." He looked over his shoulder at the bedroom door. "Don't go like this."

"I'm sorry," I said, backing away from him. "This has been a mistake. It's just opened up all those old wounds, all that old pain."

He grasped my hand and pressed it to his lips before wrapping his arms around my waist. "Does this feel like a mistake?" He said, his lips brushing against mine. Tears poured down my face but I didn't pull away.

"This is not a mistake, Shea," he said. I felt myself melting into him, my legs weak with desire.

"Don't leave," he whispered, pulling away from me, brushing a hair off my forehead. "I want to make love to you every day. I want to forget that we ever lost each other.

I don't care what happened back then. It's the past. We've grown up."

"You don't care what happened?" My jaw dropped my heart raced. "You crushed me Troy," I said. "When you left you destroyed me."

"I told you I'm sorry," he said. "I should never have given up on us."

"I waited for you," I said. "I waited at that courthouse for hours until it was dark."

His face paled. "I never . . ." He whispered.

"You are asking too much of me," I said. "Too much."

I backed away from him.

"Shea wait!" he called.

I ran down the stairs and out the front door sobbing. I never looked back, not once.

CHAPTER 13

The house was empty when I got home. I was grateful for the silence. I called Odessa but she didn't answer, then I remembered her texting something about going out of town for a few days.

I cracked open a hard cider and sat on the front porch. I felt lost and alone.

I had tricked myself into believing for three gorgeous days that I could go back in time and erase the past. Hearing Troy explain his plan for developing our hometown and buying out my family, forced me to recognize that we were different people.

If he really understood me or my family, he would have known that we could never sell this land. I felt like I'd fallen for the wrong guy all over. Once again I was the fool with a broken heart.

I squinted as headlights came down the drive. It was Caiden's police cruiser. He and Max stepped out of the car and walked towards the house.

"You okay?" Caiden asked right away. He was always so good at reading me.

"No," I said, taking another swig of my cider.

Caiden sat down beside me and wrapped his arm

around my shoulder.

Max leaned over and kissed the top of my head. "Looks like little sister needs a strong drink," he said.

"I don't really think more alcohol is going to help here," I sniffed.

"Oh come now, do not under estimate the power of a fabulous old-fashioned. Soon you'll be fit as a fiddle." He grinned at his clever alliteration. "You in Caiden?"

"No thanks," Caiden said. "I'm on the clock."

"How's dad," I said, leaning against Caiden's shoulder.

"He's fine and you're not crying over Dad," Caiden said.

"I'm not crying," I said, wiping tears off my cheek.

A few minutes later the kitchen door opened and Max walked out holding two clinking glasses. "Just what the doctor ordered."

I laughed and took one of the cool drinks. "You do not prescribe old-fashioneds to your patients."

"No, but I should," Max said. "Do you know how many people could do with just relaxing in this world? Just taking things a little less seriously? Everybody is so dramatic."

"Shea is sad," Caiden said, kicking his twin in the leg.

"Oh shit, sorry, what's up little sister," Max said. "Do

I need to kick Troy's ass?"

"No," I said, stifling a sob. "It's bad."

"How bad?" Caiden asked.

"Really bad," I said. "Troy wants Dad to sell. He says if he doesn't the bank is going to foreclose."

"Foreclose?" Caiden said, his voice soft.

"Bullshit," Max said.

"Troy said he has stalled the bank somehow to buy time, but if the foreclosure moves forward and his company finds out about it, Dad won't get a good price. He wants dad to make a deal soon so he doesn't end up losing everything."

"Well that won't really matter if he loses this place," Max said, sighing and tipping back his drink. "If he loses this land, it will kill him. You don't have to be a doctor to see that."

My vision blurred and my breath shook as I took a drink.

Caiden stared into the distance, his lips drawn in a tight line as if he were looking at something he didn't like. "You aren't surprised," I said.

"Nope," Caiden said. "Ben's in trouble. I was hoping I was wrong. He and Daisy had a good run together earlier in the year, but this last break up was hard on him. Without her, I think he's just drifting and clearly he doesn't feel like he can come to any of us for help."

"Great," I snorted. "I get left at the altar and basically get disowned when I leave town, Ben breaks up with someone and loses the orchard. We are ridiculous."

"She is right," Max said. "We are horrible children, just horrible." That was Max, finding inappropriate humor at our darkest hour.

"Well, we're not so horrible that we can't fix it." Caiden stood up, his walkie-talkie buzzed and beeped with conversation. "All right well, we aren't fixing this tonight. I have to go back to the station. You want a ride Max?"

"Yeah, thanks. I want to check on Mom and then head home," Max said, throwing back the rest of his drink.

"Thanks for telling us Shea," Caiden said. "Let Max and I deal with the bank and with Ben."

"No, I want to help this time," I said, jumping to my feet drink in hand. I followed them into the drive. "You two are always handling things."

"You have your life in Seattle," Max said, waiting for Caiden to let him into the cruiser. "Escape this mess little sister. Be free. Caiden and I will figure it out. You go to sleep. We'll keep you posted."

"But you've all known for months that things aren't

right here," I said, standing. "Dad's been in decline. Ben seems depressed as hell. Troy is back and no one told me. Not one of you."

Caiden leaned over the roof of his car, keys in hand. "We were trying to protect you Shea."

"But I don't need protection!" I said, my hands balled into fists. I hadn't meant to shout. "I'm a grown woman. I can handle this."

"All right then," Caiden said. He and Max exchanged a look between them.

"The lady has spoken," Max said, doing a tiny mock bow.

"Forget it. You two drive me crazy," I muttered turning and heading toward the house.

"But you love us," Max called after me.

"Still drive me crazy!" I shouted waving them off.

"Wait until tomorrow," Caiden called out. "We'll come by in the afternoon."

"Dude I have to check my surgery schedule," Max said, holding his hands up into the air. "The hands may have a command performance."

"All right, well, we'll figure out a time later," Caiden said.

"Fine," I said, my heart pounding. My brothers did not

get it. We needed to move faster, I wanted answers now. "Talk tomorrow," I said, choosing my words carefully.

"Good girl," Max said, blowing me a kiss and climbing into the car.

Good girl? I shrugged and waved giving them my best smile. Good girl? I preferred smart girl.

I stood on the front steps and waved like a good little sister as my brothers drove away. They wanted me to wait until morning. Right. I didn't think so.

It wasn't that I'd just lied to my brothers. It was more like I'd held back a little bit when I agreed to do nothing for a while.

I was tired of all the men in my life telling me to back off and let them handle everything. Troy wanted to rescue us, which really meant he was trying to rescue me. His solution was horrible, but once again he wanted me to just let him fix everything. And now Caiden and Max seemed to think that they needed to be at the helm to right our family's ship.

I walked back into the house and pounded my old-fashioned. The whiskey bloomed in my belly as I opened the door to my father's office. It was time for me to quit asking so many questions and get some answers for myself.

CHAPTER 14

I went through two full file cabinets of paperwork before I dropped my head to the top of my father's desk in defeat. The files were an organizational nightmare. All the contracts were out of date and shoved into folders every which way. There was one whole drawer devoted to old farm and appliance manuals including an old Cuisinart which I knew for a fact had broken at least fifteen years ago.

No bank statements. No tax documents. No ledgers. My head throbbed above my left eyebrow. No wonder this place was falling apart. Once upon a time when my Dad had done the books, I'd sat by him at the kitchen counter watching him move numbers from column to column in his big leather book.

Seeing him be so hands on was one of the reasons I insisted on balancing my own books every month instead of handing off the job to an accountant.

Had Dad let go of control because he could no longer manage the place? Or was stepping back his way of showing faith in Ben. What would my father do if it turned out his faith and trust had been misplaced?

I rubbed my temple. I needed to find the ledger if the

old artifact still existed. I had rifled through every nook and cranny in this place except one. Standing in the corner of the room stood an old-school wooden file cabinet and all the drawers were locked.

I held a letter opener in my hands and eyed that cabinet wondering how far I was willing to go for answers. I might be able to pry my way in, but I'd destroy those antique drawers in the process.

I closed my eyes, weary for sleep and wondering if Caiden and Max were right. Maybe I should just back away from this mess and let them solve it.

Troy had a proposal for my family. Granted I thought it was a terrible proposal, but if things were as bad as he thought, maybe it was the right thing to do. Negotiate now and let Troy help Mom and Dad get the best price for their property.

The idea of packing up my parents made me want to throw up on myself.

"I am wasting my time," I said out loud. "Wasting my time and sticking my nose in places I'm not wanted."

"Who says you aren't wanted?" I heard Mom's voice behind me.

"Hi," I said, spinning around on Dad's office chair. "So, I was just . . ." I struggled for words. There was no good way to explain why I was sitting in Dad's office surrounded by an explosion of paper and open drawers.

"You find what you were looking for honey?"

"No," I said, covering my eyes. "I'm snooping and I feel horrible and I don't know what to do. If I believe my lying ex-boyfriend, our family is in big trouble. If I believe my older brother who has devoted his life to this place, then my ex is using me to get what he wants. Both options are horrible mom." I peeked out at her from between my fingers.

She didn't look angry, in fact she looked thoughtful as she leaned her head against the doorframe.

"Your ex has a name sweetheart. You can say his name."

"Fine," I said. "Troy. Troy says we have big troubles." I still couldn't bring myself to say the word foreclosure in front of her. I already felt that Dad's health problems had aged her enough.

"And what does your heart tell you?"

"My heart?"

"Your heart, your gut, either way you think of it, you must be leaning one way more than the other."

"My heart," I sighed and rubbed my temple. "I feel like a jerk for doubting Ben, but I think Troy may be right. Then again, I've been wrong about Troy in the past, what if I'm wrong now?"

"Honey, I believe him too," Mom said, her voice soft.

"You do?"

"Max came by the hospital so I could go to evening Mass."

"Mom, I should have done that for you. Max was here, he should have told me," I said, feeling guilty for being so self-absorbed.

"I'm not telling you to make you feel guilty honey," Mom said. "I was too late for the Sunday night service, but I did go to church to pray. I kept replaying your conversation with Ben this morning. Something didn't sit right with me about it and I couldn't quite say why. Do you remember what he said when you asked him if the orchard was in trouble?"

"He told me things are fine."

"No," Mom said, pointing her finger at me. "He said it's his problem and not to worry. He never answered you sweetheart."

Mom was right. I remembered the way Ben had looked at me, so angry and defensive. "You think he didn't want to tell the truth."

"Your brother isn't perfect honey, but there is one

thing Ben isn't," Mom said. "He isn't a liar. I've been hoping that Ben would find his place for some time. I've even talked to your Dad about it, but he's never wanted to believe that Ben was anything but happy taking over these orchards."

"He sure doesn't seem happy," I said. "Why can't Dad see that?"

"Because sometimes he sees what he wants to see. Your dad grew up wanting to run this place just like his Daddy. I think he just assumed that Ben was just like him."

I smiled at Mom and wondered if I would ever get the chance to love my own children the way she loved us. She seemed to have mastered that art of unconditional love without putting us up on pedestals where we were doomed to fall. Once upon a time I'd wanted children with Troy, I reminded myself.

I took a breath. It was difficult not to get lost in the memory of making love to that man, then and now. We had great sex, mind blowing sex, oh-my-God-I-want-him-again-sex, but that didn't mean we shared the kind of love we needed to have a family together.

"You thinking about Troy?" Mom asked.

"No," I said, trying to play it off. "I was thinking about the orchard."

His Three Piece Suit

"You do this thing where you bite your lip and look all day dreamy when you think of him," Mom said.

I blanched and put on my best poker face. "Do not."

"Do too honey, it's the reason I wasn't totally surprised the morning you two tried to run away together. Love was written all over your face."

"You knew?" I said, my heart pounding. I had thought I was being so sneaky that morning. I'd lied and made up a story about needing to help Paul with summer school. Instead, I'd packed my bag and left a note for Mom and Dad on my pillow knowing they wouldn't find it until nightfall long after Troy and I had said "I do."

"I'll say this. If I had known for sure where you were going that morning, I would have barred the door. But when Paul showed up and exposed your lie, I remembered the way you'd looked all morning and I knew you and Troy had made big plans."

"Mom, I'm so sorry I lied to you and Dad that day. And the note I left," I cringed remembering my teenage melodrama.

"Honey, I'm glad that all happened."

"Glad?"

"I knew heartbreak like that would make you rethink your life, what you wanted to do, what you wanted to be.

You weren't ready to marry Troy and end up spending the rest of your life on this side of the mountains. You were half-baked honey. You weren't you yet and neither was Troy. You both needed more time."

"I thought we would be together forever," I whispered.

"I'm not so sure honey. Look at who you have become. You've moved away. Started your own business. You aren't the quiet girl who was afraid of the world when you fell in love with that boy."

"I wasn't quiet," I said.

"Weren't quiet," Mom said, rolling her eyes. "You were my runner, the one who would take to the hills to think when things got rough."

"I still do that."

"Yes, but you aren't afraid to ask questions now, to dig for answers. That heartbreak made you who you are today, honey. Every hurt makes us stronger and braver and Lord knows it takes bravery to face life some times."

"I don't feel brave," I whispered.

"Not brave," Mom snorted. "Let me ask you something. Do your brothers know you are in here snooping?"

"No," I said, cringing. "And I feel like a liar, not a hero."

"Give yourself some credit honey," Mom said. "You are standing up for your family. It's time I stood up too."

"What do you mean?"

"It's time for answers."

"There aren't any here. I've gone through every scrap of paper in this place and I can't get into that antique cabinet without breaking the lock."

"About that," Mom said, holding a gold key in the air. I recognized it right away as the charm she usually wore on a chain around her neck.

"That's a real key?" I gasped.

"Your Dad has one key. I have the other and I always thought it was pretty so it's been around my neck for years."

"And in all that time, you've never gone through these drawers."

"Of course not. Your Dad gave me this key when you kids were little so I could give it to the attorney's if anything ever happened to him. It wasn't for me, it was a safeguard in case he died."

"But he's not dead."

"No he's not, but it's about time he realized that his bench is deeper than he thinks." Mom unlocked the cabinet and handed me a stack of manila folders. "Let's get to work girl."

CHAPTER 15

Inside that file cabinet, I found my Dad's old bank ledgers and stacks of bank statements detailing the monthly draws on savings and the dwindling deposits.

It didn't take an MBA to figure out what was going on with the property.

Less profit. More loss.

Mom poured through pages of dad's old ledgers running her fingers over the grid where he'd painstakingly tracked every invoice paid.

"He kept the house in order for a long time," Mom said, a wistful smile on her face. "He should have let me help him more."

"He didn't think he needed you Mom," I said, trying not to sound sour. "He had Ben."

"Shea, your brother did a lot of good here for a long time," Mom said. "I should have stayed involved."

"And Ben should have said he was in trouble."

"Honey, just because someone is a grown-up doesn't mean they have the good sense to ask for help." Mom sighed and returned to her books. It was clear the orchards were losing money but I still hadn't found any statements from the bank, there was nothing to suggest that we were inching towards that horrible word *foreclosure.*

Finally, I found an unmarked folder lying flat on the bottom of a drawer. Someone had clearly stashed this folder in a place where it wouldn't be easily found.

"Got it," I said, jumping up and scanning the stack of documents inside. "Looks like we started to have some trouble with the mortgage on the North and South fields about a year ago. I see partial payments, a couple months of full payments and then nothing for the past six months. It's bad, but maybe we can cover this loss."

Mom swiveled around on her chair, her face pale. "What did you say?"

"The mortgage," I said, handing her one of the more recent statements. "Troy said we were behind on payments, and he is right but it seems like the real trouble started six months ago. I didn't want to tell you but he claimed the bank was going to foreclose."

"That land was paid for on your sixteenth birthday," Mom said, her hand shaking as she held the statement. "Your father and I celebrated with a steak dinner at the Gold Digger. We toasted the fact that we'd never be beholden to the bank again."

"I'm sorry Mom," I said.

The statements were all damning. Month after month

of inconsistent payments, followed by no payments at all for six months.

"Why did he mortgage the land without telling me?" Mom said, her eyes filling with tears.

"I don't know. The orchard has not made money for years. Dad and Ben must have been strapped for cash and thought this was the only option. Dad never mentioned anything about needing a new mortgage?"

"No. He hates credit. He knows it's a part of business, but he's never been comfortable," Mom squinted her eyes as if trying to remember something. "You know your Dad did mention getting Ben added to our accounts a while back. I signed a stack of paperwork about a year ago, but I can't imagine that I signed off on a new loan." Mom looked up at me, tears glistening in her eyes. "I should never have allowed myself to be in the dark like this. I should have asked more questions."

I held my mom as she cried, her head on my shoulder. I stroked her hair and I told her that everything would be all right. We would find a way I promised. We would not be defeated.

I thought about Troy's offer. Was this our only way out? The idea made me feel trapped and angry. Troy didn't know how hard my family had worked over the years. He didn't understand what it was like to grow up on this land. Holding my mother, I felt that if Troy were truly the man I belonged with he would never have asked my parent's to give up on their dream.

"I'm so sorry it wasn't good news," I told her.

Mom looked up at me, her eyes full of pain, but still she smiled. "It doesn't matter that it wasn't good," she said, giving my hand a squeeze. "It's the truth. And knowing the truth is always better than burying your head in the sand."

"But it feels bad."

"Sure it does," Mom said, grabbing a tissue and drying her eyes. "But now that we know what we are up against. Now we can figure a way out. Tell me about Troy's offer."

"Mom," I said. "I don't want to go there."

"Shea Marie I need to know everything that is on the table and you do too."

So, I told Mom about the Salishan Cabana project and the plan to take over our orchards and replace them with a vineyard.

"Apparently the soil has the perfect pH level for growing grapes," I said. "Troy's partners want to turn our land into a working vineyard and tasting room so they have their world class resort."

Mom massaged her forehead. "We don't have the cash

to fight this," she said. "I have some money saved up, but not enough. Even then, what happens the next month, and the month after. You said it yourself the orchard hasn't made money in years."

"Troy knows about the mortgage," I said. "He knows we are behind but he has kept that information from his partners."

"So, they don't know yet?" Mom whispered.

"Not yet," I said. I had to tell her everything, it was time to go all in. "I feel sick even telling you this, but he thinks we should sell now. He says he can negotiate a price that allows you and Dad to buy something else. He says if we move right now, he can help us."

"I see," she said. "And if they realize how bad off we are . . ." her voice trailed off.

"They'll buy the land as cheaply as they can and he won't be able to help us," I shrugged. "Or worse, they buy it from the bank."

"I see," Mom repeated. She sighed and brushed her hair off her forehead before standing. "It is time for sleep," She said. "We aren't solving anything tonight."

"But we need an answer soon," I said.

"Yes we do sweetheart, yes we do," Mom kissed me.

"Night." I kissed her back and tried to fight the tears

filling my eyes as she turned to go.

"Troy is right Shea," Mom said, standing in the doorway. "Thank him for helping me face the truth in my family. I have known something isn't right and I've been hiding from it, telling myself that my instincts are wrong. Thank him for helping me to see."

"I will," I whispered, hugging my arms.

I closed up the office putting everything back in place the way I'd found it. Then I stood at the foot of the stairs listening to the quiet.

Troy was right.

I let that statement sink in for a moment. I tried the idea on for size and liked how it fit.

Troy had been trying to help my family and I'd doubted him based on my wounded pride. It was true that Troy had broken my heart years ago, but I was the one who came home as rarely as possible, who dialed it in at the holidays barely engaging. I always had one foot out the door the moment I arrived in Salishan. I said it was work, but the truth was I made up reasons to stay away.

Mom seemed to think that I'd come into my own over the last ten years and in some ways she was right, but I think she'd let me off too easy when it came to my family. Troy had hurt me, but how I dealt with that hurt was my choice, it always had been. The truth was I hadn't been paying attention to the people who loved me most. I'd let my family down.

Mom was right the truth wasn't always pretty. In fact, sometimes it was downright ugly but it was always better than living a lie.

Dad no longer was in charge and Ben was in no shape to take control.

I had a choice. Go upstairs and do nothing, or find a way to fix it.

With my hand on the bannister, I stared up those stairs knowing that sleep was just a few steps away. I could go upstairs and climb into bed and wait for my brothers to help sort out this mess.

Or, I could do something.

I took a breath and turned around headed back to the office. If I was going to find a way out of this mess, I needed to get to work.

CHAPTER 16

I woke with my face plastered against a stack of bank statement on Dad's desk. The sweet smell of fresh baked scones drifted into the office from the kitchen and I figured that Mom was baking out her troubles.

The clock on the wall read 7:00 a.m.

I sat up with a start and powered up the old laptop I'd found in the bottom drawer of the desk. My spreadsheet was open with the cursor blinking.

I checked my numbers one more time. Back and forth. I reconciled the statements making sure the books balanced. If this was going to work, I needed to know exactly how much cash we had on hand and how much we owed.

Then I flipped open the word document I'd started after Mom went to bed. I hit print and held my breath as the ancient printer in the office came to life. Well thank God my Dad wasn't a total luddite. He may not have used technology but at least he had some in the office.

I paced as the document printed out, page after page.

If I was right, I may have found a way to bring us back. If I was wrong . . .

The printer quieted as the last sheet whoosh'd into the tray. I grabbed a manila folder stuffed all my paperwork

167

inside before running down the hall.

"Mom?" I called, sliding across the hardwood floor in my socks.

"Shea!" Mom said. "You'll fall . . ." She stood at the counter, her arms deep in a bowl kneading more dough. The countertop looked like a professional bakery with trays of scones cooling and dough ready for the oven.

"I know how to fix it Mom," I said, pointing to the folder.

"Fix it. What do you mean, fix it?" Mom said, eyes wide, her tone excited but tinged with fear. She took her hands out of the dough and picked up a towel cleaning her sticky fingers.

"Go get dressed," I said. "Wear something nice. We are going to the bank."

"The bank?" Mom said, smoothing down the pocket of her robe.

"We've got some business to do," I said, heading out of the kitchen. "I'll explain on the way."

"All right then," Mom said, her face breaking out in a smile, cheeks flushed. "Let's do this," she said, running up the stairs.

I watched her go and took a breath. I had one more thing I needed to do before getting dressed. I picked up my phone and dialed without hesitating.

"Shea," Troy answered, right away. "I wanted to call you all night . . ."

"We can talk later about us," I said, closing my eyes, hoping and praying my plan would work. "I called you for another reason."

"Oh," he said, sounding disappointed.

"Can you meet my mother and me at Cascade Bank?" I said. "I need your help."

* * * *

Standing in the parking lot of Cascade Bank next to Troy and Mom. I laid out all the paperwork on the hood of Dad's truck and walked them through my plan.

"What do you think? I asked, picking up the pages one by one. My hands shook from nerves and adrenaline and probably lack of sleep.

Troy nodded and exhaled. "Well . . ."

"Well what?" I said, my heart racing. I looked back and forth between the two of them. "If you don't think it will work, tell me now. Just spit it out."

"It's risky," Troy said, breaking into a lopsided grin. "But it's the good kind of risk. I think it's solid Shea. You've done your homework." Eyes wide, he nodded his head and ran his fingers through his hair.

"Hardly . . ." I said. "I feel like I'm coming off of an all-night cram session in college. I need to know if you are both in."

"We're in," Mom blurted. I had given her a run down in the car already so this was her second time through the plan. "I mean I'm in sweetheart, I'm in. I can't speak for Troy, of course."

"I'm in too," Troy said. He reached out and grasped my hand looking me straight in the eyes. "I'm all in. Shea I want to tell you . . ."

"Not now," I said, squeezing his hand. Just touching him made me feel a bit weak. "You and I will sort everything out later, I promise. I need to focus. It's time for my A game."

"Right." Troy nodded and grinned at me while Mom pretended to be distracted by a passing cloud.

"Okay then," I said. I took a breath and threw back my shoulders. "You all ready?"

They nodded.

"Good. Follow my lead."

We all walked into the bank.

✻ ✻ ✻ ✻

"Mary O'Toole." Earl Bishop, the manager of Cascade Bank got up from his desk in the back office. Earl's kids had gone to school with the twins. Earl was bald as a cue ball and looked red-faced and flustered as he scooted out from behind his desk. "I've been praying for William," he said, clasping his hands. "We've all been so worried about him. Such a stressful time, so stressful." He glanced at Troy and took a step back. "Well, hello Mr. Van Rossum." His eyes darted from Troy to us. "Surprised to see you here of course."

Troy had said that he'd interfered on our behalf at the bank. It was clear from Mr. Bishop's expression that he was surprised to see us walking into the bank together.

"Mr. Bishop," I said, stepping in front of Troy. "My mother and I are here to talk to you about our land."

Mr. Bishop swallowed. "Well, maybe we should wait for William or Benjamin."

"No, we shouldn't," Mom said. "Shea is here to negotiate on behalf of our family, Mr. Bishop."

"Well then, I see," he said, clearly flustered. He eyeballed Troy and nodded his direction. "Are you sure you should be discussing this in front of you know . . ."

"Troy is here as a representative of Ardent investments and the Salishan Cabana project," I said.

"It's true," Troy said, taking out his card. "I'm here on behalf of the firm."

Mr. Bishop's eyes about bugged out of his head.

"So, I think we are ready then," I said, smiling. "Mr. Van Rossum is here to talk about investing and I'm here to talk about the fact our property is close to foreclosure."

Saying the "f" word out loud made me shake, but I took a breath. I am strong. I am brave. I am standing up for my family. I reminded myself remembering Mom's advice the night before.

I'm taking no shit and taking names.

"Maybe we should all sit down then," Mr. Bishop whispered wiping his sweaty brow with a handkerchief. "This way."

We followed him into his office and all took seats in front of his big wooden desk. I slid my business plan across the desk and started talking. It was my turn to shine.

* * * *

Thirty minutes later we had a letter of agreement and a plan to return with Dad to sign the final papers.

My hands shook as we walked out of the bank into the sunlight. I stood blinking as my eyes adjusted to the light. Troy wrapped his arms around my waist and spun me in the air laughing.

"You were amazing in there Shea." He lowered me to my feet and planted a firm kiss right on my lips.

172

His Three Piece Suit

Mom cleared her throat and I opened my eyes to see her standing beside me with a huge grin on her face. She threw her arms around both of us in a great big hug.

"Thank you both," she said, looking up with tears of joy in her eyes. "Now let's go home and tell your father what we've done."

CHAPTER 17

It was time to talk to Dad. Not even the high of having my plan pan out could dull the wave of fear that seized my body. What if Dad hated what I'd done? What if he thought I'd sold us out and betrayed the family?

I kept my fears to myself as I gripped the wheel and drove towards the farmhouse. I'd done the best I could, I reminded myself. I was standing up for our family. Everything I'd done that day had been out of love and respect for my family and the legacy they had built.

Of course, talking to Dad meant talking to Ben. I wondered if Ben would be able to see past his anger to listen to me and Mom especially when he looked out the window to see Troy Van Rossum and his fancy silver sports car.

Mom made calls as we drove. She was brief, but firm.

"We need a family meeting," she said. "No, I won't explain right now. Pick up your father and be at the house in thirty minutes or there will be hell to pay."

Troy followed us as we drove through town, past Sweet Treats bakery and along the winding road that framed the lake and finally down our drive.

"Well, that's the first time they've all listened to me at

once," Mom said, eyes wide as we in front of the house, all three of the boys' cars were already there, parked in a single line.

I inhaled, my breath shaking a little I wondered when my courage had decided to run off and turn into fear. "You think this is going to go all right?" I asked, hesitating before getting out of the car.

"I think it doesn't really matter how it goes, honey. Desperate times require desperate measures," Mom said. She reached over and squeezed my hand. "You found a way to fix things and it's about time those boys realize their little sister has grown-up and has a fine mind for business."

"Thanks Mom," I said.

"I'm proud of you Shea." Mom leaned over and kissed my cheek and we both got out of the car.

"You sure you want me there with you?" Troy asked, standing next to me in the gravel drive. "I don't want to make things harder for you."

"No," I said, reaching out to take his hand firmly in mine. "This wouldn't have been possible without you. I want you standing beside me."

"I want to stand beside you too," Troy said, his voice a little shaky. He squeezed my hand and cleared his throat.

"Let's get this over with you two," Mom said, her

expression strong and determined.

Inside Dad sat in his favorite leather chair by the fireplace with Ben by his side. Their eyes widened as Mom and I walked inside with Troy following.

"You said family meeting," Ben said, nodding at Troy.

"Troy is here on my invitation," Mom said, holding up her hand.

"What is this Mary?" Dad said, straightening up in his chair. His cheeks had more color and I was happy to see him out of his wheelchair, I only hoped the next few minutes didn't give him another heart attack.

Caiden and Max sat side by side on the couch each holding sections of the *Salishan Times*. They looked curious and a little worried.

Caiden in particular gave me a wide-eyed look which roughly translated to "What the hell are you doing little sister?"

Mom nodded at me. "Go, on now," she said, her voice soft.

I took a step forward feeling like a reluctant kid being pushed on stage to do a solo at a talent show. "So," I said. "I wanted to talk to you all."

I looked over to see Troy. He nodded at me and smiled. His face was so full of love and support I could almost hear him in my head saying, "You can do it Shea Marie, don't listen to your fear. Trust me. Trust yourself."

"Mom and I just came from Cascade bank," I said, my voice strong.

"Whoah, whoah," Ben said. The panic on his face impossible to ignore. "You need to involve me . . ." His voice rose to near shouting levels.

"No," I said. My voice firm but kind. "You need to listen to me now Ben," I said. My pulse raced and my cheeks flushed but I felt impossibly calm. There was no fear, no doubt. "I'm here to help our family and it's time for you all to hear me out."

Ben looked stunned. He took a step closer to Dad who just looked at me with a puzzled expression on his face. Then without a word Mom walked around the room, stood beside Ben and reached down to hold his hand.

"Go on Shea," she said. "We're ready."

Ben's shoulders sagged and I saw something in his eyes burn out, that spark that made him so fierce and angry disappeared, just like that. He looked from me to Mom and I could see that soft-hearted boy who used to rescue birds with broken wings in the orchard. I recognized the kind eyes of my brother who had left for University so hopeful and full of optimism. Maybe that young man wasn't lost

177

forever.

"So, there have been some issues with the property, Dad." I said, choosing my words carefully. I wanted Dad to understand the situation but humiliating my brother was not part of my plan. "Financially it seems like we've had some challenges."

"Let me tell him, Shea," Ben said, interrupting me. He let go of Mom's hand and ran a hand through his salt and pepper hair. "It's about time I tell the truth anyway. It's been weighing on me like a anvil around my neck."

"Ben," I said. "This isn't about blame . . ."

"Dad, I mortgaged the North and South orchards," Ben said.

"You what?" Dad's head popped up, eyes blinking, mouth gaping.

"We haven't been making a profit for over five years," Ben said. "I tried to talk to you about it, tried to find a way to work around it and finally we ran out of operating cash. This is my mistake. This happened under my watch."

"Lord almighty," Dad whispered, closing his eyes.

"The trouble is, the mortgage wasn't enough," Ben said. "I thought the influx of cash would come back tenfold, but all it's done is put us into debt." Ben swallowed. "I've gotten behind on the payments. The bank has started the process to foreclose."

Dad sat silent, staring straight ahead. Ben glanced from Dad to me, his eyes wide and wounded looking. "I was afraid to tell you," he said, looking at me. "Afraid to tell all of you. I was ashamed of not being straight with the family about the loan, even more ashamed it didn't work out."

"I know something about feeling ashamed, Ben," I said, my eyes filling with tears. "What's done is done. We aren't allowed to hit rewind in this life, as much as we want to." I glanced back at Troy standing behind me. I wanted to make sure he had heard me.

"We have a way out," I said. "I have managed to save a good chunk of money, enough to make a lump sum payment and temporarily stop the foreclosure proceedings."

"No," Dad said, sitting up taller. "Shea Marie, that is your business."

"I may have moved to the other side of the mountains, but this place is still my home and I would never have been able to run my own business if you hadn't taught me how."

Dad opened his mouth to protest.

"Please Daddy," I said. "I am a part of this family and I need you to let me help. Just listen."

Dad closed his mouth shut and nodded.

"If the bank backs off it gives us time to reevaluate our business. Reevaluate what this town needs. Which brings in Troy."

Ben looked at Troy, his eyes narrowing.

"I know you all think he's here to take our land away and change our way of life, but the thing is Salishan is going to change whether Troy's here or not."

"I am so sorry if you thought my offer to buy you out was disrespectful," Troy said. "I have had nothing but respect for this land and your family since the first day I set foot on this orchard."

"Troy's firm wants to invest in our property, turn the Southern orchard into a vineyard," I said. "The bank has agreed to renegotiate the terms of our mortgage and give us enough money to convert those apple fields to grapes."

"A winery," Ben said, his eyes wide.

"Tear them out," Dad murmured.

"We tear out the apples and plant the grapes. Build a tasting room for the tourists," I said, my voice racing with energy. "Mom is on board to run the place and I was thinking that Ben you might want to design the out buildings. Weren't you studying architecture before you dropped out of school?"

"I haven't thought about that in years," Ben said. He

nodded at me and quickly looked away. I wasn't sure but I thought I saw the glint of tears in his eyes.

"Who will come to a winery out here?" Dad asked, looking flustered.

"The Salishan Cabana project is breaking ground in a month," Troy said. "The development across the road is going to be there whether or not you make a change. The people will come."

"Doesn't your firm want to own the operation?" Ben asked. For once his question didn't sound like an accusation. He sounded respectful and genuinely curious.

"My firm's primary investment is the vacation properties," Troy said. "As long as the area includes the type of experiences they think will help people come here and buy, they are willing to invest as a minor shareholder."

"How Minor?" Dad asked, perking up in his seat.

"10 percent," Troy said, smiling. "I tried to get your daughter to agree to 20 percent but she's a pretty tough negotiator."

"We don't need that much of their capital," I said. "10 percent will do just fine and Ardent is a totally silent partner. We control our land. The investment gives us marketing power, it gets us included in the Salishan Cabana brochures and activity lists. They'll even sell custom vacation packages that include tasting menus and cases of wine."

"I think it's brilliant," Max said, nodding from his spot in the corner. "We keep the Northern orchard in apples and diversify. I for one would love to be a part of the grape business. You know how I love my wine." Max winked, but he was being truthful.

"I'm in too," Caiden said. "I'm in and I'd like to help Dad. And from the way Mom and Ben are smiling, I think it seems that the people who work here like the idea?"

"Me too," I said. "I want to help. I know about marketing and drumming up business."

"Ben," Dad said, taking a breath. "What do you think we should do?"

Ben took a breath, his chest shaking as he spoke. "This is exactly the kind of change and innovation that this family needs Dad. I can run this. I can make this work."

Troy moved beside me and held my hand. I hadn't even realized that my hands were shaking until I felt him beside me.

"The truth is, a lot of this on me," Dad said.

"No, Dad . . ." Ben started.

"Hold on son." Dad held up his hand. "I am the head of this household and I know I haven't been as hands on recently as I should have been, but this goes back a long time."

Dad sighed and pursed his lips for a moment. "I love this land, but I love this family more and change is not easy for me. You may have noticed."

We all laughed.

"A long time ago, Shea Marie, you wrote a note and left this family. That was change, or a reminder to me that change was coming no matter how much I wanted to keep my little girl with me." Dad looked up at me, his voice caught.

"Dad," I said, tears pouring down my cheeks faster than I'd expected.

"I was afraid I'd lost you that day and instead of figuring out how to make peace with that feeling, I shut you out sweetheart." Dad held out his hand to me. "I shut you out and what I should have done is pull you close. Moving away from home, finding your way, none of those things are bad. It's what you do in this life. You needed to grow up and fall in love." He nodded at Troy. "That's the best thing that can ever happen to a father, it's a joy to see your daughter so happy and with a good man."

"Oh dad," I ran to my father and he pulled me into a hug, a real one, that felt like he meant it.

I looked up to see Troy standing in place, eyes wide. He nodded, "Thank you sir," he said, his voice strong and full of emotion.

"And then with this orchard, I just always expected you to take things over, Ben."

"I always wanted to do that Dad," Ben said.

"Did you son?" Dad looked at Ben his eyes narrowing. "I had completely forgotten that you'd even started college until Shea mentioned how you'd studied architecture."

"It was a long time ago," Ben said.

"It was, but it's not too late for you to finish that degree," Dad said. "If we build this winery it can't just be on your shoulders son. Mary I think you should run the place."

"You got it," Mom said.

"I want this family to speak their mind and follow their hearts," Dad said, his voice full and booming. I swear I saw more of the color return to his cheeks. "I love you kids, but I want each and every one of you to not be afraid to go after your dreams, to follow your hearts."

"Thanks Dad," I whispered.

Mom moved beside him and leaned over and kissed him straight on the mouth a little longer than usual.

"Get a room already," Max shouted.

His Three Piece Suit

Dad grinned. "Ben," he said, motioning to my brother. "It's time you and I had a talk, a real honest one."

"Yes, sir," Ben said.

"How about you call me Dad."

"All right, Dad," Ben said.

"So, tell me," Dad said, looking straight into my brother's eyes. "What would you like to do with your life, son?"

Ben sat beside Dad that afternoon and they talked, their voices a low murmur of tears and laughter. I think all those years of never choosing poured out of my brother and Dad listened for once to his oldest son. We all gave them space and privacy since I think we all knew that to unravel ten years of sadness takes time.

Ben had forgotten how to speak up for himself, how to listen to his gut and the calling of his heart's dream.

I squeezed Troy's hand in mine and resolved to never ignore my heart again. My heart was standing beside me and I never wanted to let him go.

CHAPTER 18

We spent the day with my family making plans and pulling all the necessary paperwork together for the final loan application. Mom had her hands all over Dad's office, shredding useless documents and bringing some order to the chaos. I was pretty sure the days of locked file cabinets were done for the family business.

Max had made a wine run and set up a mock tasting room at the kitchen table sampling different blends with an assortment of Mom's baked goods. It was Caiden's day off so he let loose a little. His cheeks flushed, he raised a Dixie cup of wine in the air and sniffed it before taking a drink, followed by a bite of one of Mom's chocolate chip cookies.

I didn't expect either of my brothers to give up their day jobs, but I know it warmed my Dad's heart to see them making a contribution to our family's future.

"Make sure you work out a payment plan for Shea Marie that includes a reasonable interest rate," Dad said, reviewing the spreadsheets. Troy and I had done one more run of the numbers to be sure there would be no surprises when we secured our financing.

"Dad, that's not necessary," I said.

"You are getting this family out of trouble. You've

worked hard to launch your business and I don't expect your career to suffer as a result," Dad smiled.

"You don't need to pay me interest."

"What's the matter, you afraid we won't be in the black?" Dad said, teasing.

"Not a bit."

"Listen to your father and take the money, Shea," Troy said, nudging me.

"Smart man."

"Find a reasonable rate," I agreed.

Dad glanced at the clock on the mantle. "Say, aren't you two getting a little tired of hanging out here? Don't you have somewhere you need to be?"

It was about 10:00 p.m.

"Um . . ." I wasn't sure what he was inferring.

"Go on, get out of here," Dad said, shooing us away. "Good night you two."

You could have knocked me over with a feather, my Dad was practically shoving me out the front door and into Troy's bed.

"Night Dad," I said, kissing Dad on the cheek, and grabbing Troy's hand.

"See you in the morning," Mom called from her seat at the tasting table. She and the boys had just sliced into a gorgeous looking chocolate torte that was almost delicious enough to tempt me into staying, almost.

"Good night sir," Troy said, reaching out to shake Dad's hand.

"Good night, son."

Max jumped up from the table. He gave me a hug and a chocolate crumb covered kiss on the cheek. "Don't do anything I wouldn't do," he whispered.

"Drive safe," Caiden said, as we walked through the kitchen.

Ben sat at the breakfast bar, papers spread out on the counter. He was positively beaming. He'd spent part of the day doing online research into resuming his course work and the rest of the time sketching out possible looks for a tasting room. He knew we'd have to partner with a licensed architect for the build, but he seemed giddy at the idea he could be a part of the vision and design.

"Hey Shea," he said, sliding a notepad my way as Troy and I headed towards the door. "What do you think?"

The sketch was remarkably detailed. With a soaring roof and strong beams, the building looked like a blend between a traditional and modern farmhouse. It was elegant and welcoming.

"It's amazing," I said, wondering how my brother had

come up with something that creative so quickly.

"It's rough, and I have no idea if it's structurally sound, but it's a start." He grinned, looking genuinely happy and proud. "It's been a long time since I've thought about ceiling heights and spans."

"You're talented," I said, and I meant it.

"I was thinking I might head out of here later and show Daisy," Ben said, holding his sketch in his hand. "She used to encourage me to keep this up and I didn't listen. I'd like her to see this."

"You should show her Ben." I leaned over and gave my big brother a hug, tears clouding my vision. "Don't give up on her," I whispered in his ear. "She hasn't given up on you. I promise."

Ben stared at me his eyes wide. I could see the wheels turning in his head as Troy and I walked out the front door.

"I can't wait to take you home," Troy leaned over, his voice low against my ear.

With just a few words that man had the ability to make me wet with desire. "How fast can you drive," I said, giggling.

"Real fast," Troy said. "Climb in."

* * * *

The whole drive home I replayed the day's events in

my mind. The conversation with Mr. Bishop at the bank, Ben's confession about the mortgage and Dad's agreement that something at the orchard needed to change.

Stealing glances at Troy, I realized that I couldn't imagine any of this happening without him by my side. We'd been apart for ten years. I'd spent so much time thinking it was wasted time, when maybe that distance had been exactly what we needed.

"What you thinking about?" Troy asked. He reached over and massaged my knee as he drove. His touch left me tingling for more. His fingertips felt electric every time they brushed against me.

"Nothing I'm just so happy," I said. I leaned back and closed my eyes imagining Troy's mouth against mine, the feeling of his lips sliding down my body, the sensation of his hands on my thighs as I opened my legs.

We parked in front of his house. The moment he opened my door we were all over each other. His mouth was against mine as we stumbled backwards towards the front door.

"I want you," he said, his voice husky with lust. I brushed my hand against his crotch. He was hard and throbbing.

"Yes," I gasped, as we tumbled through the front door.

His Three Piece Suit

The lights were off and moonlight filled the foyer.

We dropped our clothes across the marble floor and up the stairs, the same way we had that summer long ago. We stood naked before each other.

I dropped to my knees in front of him and reached for his hard cock. I took him in my hand and then gently kissed his tip and his shaft. He moved closer and his breathing changed as I took him in my mouth slowly. With every thrust in my mouth, I imagined my legs spreading. I wanted to make love to every part of his body.

He pushed into me and then held still. "Wait, wait," he murmured, his fingers in my hair. He withdrew himself and took my hand lifting me to my feet. Then he picked me up and laid me down on the padded window box that faced the lake.

He lowered his head between my legs, kissing me softly and gently. Rain pattered on the windows, the wind rattled the glass. Troy touched me with such tenderness and care. I relaxed completely as he coaxed my body forward. Pleasure built moment by moment, like gentle waves of water before a storm.

My body tensed with every kiss, every nibble.

"I will never get tired of watching you come," he said, looking up at me.

"And I will never get tired of feeling you inside me," I said, reaching for him I pulled him towards me and opened up my legs as he unwrapped a condom. He slid inside me gasping and moaning. The heat between us was so intense, our bodies moved together as if we were one being. He rocked forward and I opened up even more.

Breathless.

Beautiful.

Tender.

We moved faster and faster in time, in perfect unison. Our breathing aligned, our eyes open, I stared into his beautiful blue eyes as my body welcomed him in.

One more thrust.

One more moan.

He pushed inside me throbbing and quivering, the pressure of his body aligning perfectly with my aching clit. I leaned into him and felt his orgasm shaking and mine followed rolling and rippling.

We came together in the moonlight and it felt like the first time.

✳ ✳ ✳ ✳

Afterwards, Troy took my hand and we walked on shaking legs to his bed. He pulled back the covers and I slid beneath the sheets nestling my head in the crook of his arm.

He kissed the top of my head.

"I thought making love to you was the most beautiful thing in the world," he whispered. "But it's just holding you as you sleep."

"Yes, sleep," I said. "Sleep is beautiful. I'm afraid to sleep," I murmured feeling drowsy and content.

"Afraid?" He asked, kissing my temple.

"Afraid it's just a dream," I said. "Please be here when I wake."

"I'll be here every morning Shea Marie, every morning that you'll have me."

* * * *

For the first time since we were young lovers, Troy and I spent the night in each other's arms. I don't remember ever sleeping so soundly.

I awoke to the smell of fresh coffee and sunlight filtering through the curtains in his bedroom.

The moment I opened my eyes I knew exactly where I was. Even back at the farmhouse I often woke feeling unsettled as my mind raced to figure out why I wasn't in my tiny one bedroom back at the Holiday.

This was Troy's bedroom. This was the place where we'd made love the night before. This was where I belonged.

I rolled over to see a white robe folded on the nightstand along with a note.

Come downstairs my love—1+2+3 Troy.

I smiled at his reference to our old secret code.

It had been so long since I'd seen that written down. 1+2+3 = I Love you.

I climbed out of bed and pulled on a robe. I followed the sound of clanking pans and the scent of fresh coffee to the kitchen.

Troy had set the breakfast table coffee, orange juice, and a plate of scrambled eggs.

"I wasn't sure what you liked in the morning," he said, smiling when I walked into the kitchen.

"I like you in the morning," I said, walking towards him and pulling him towards me for a kiss. Troy wore a grey t-shirt and a pair of plaid pajama bottoms.

"Don't tempt me," he murmured.

"Who's tempting?" I said, flashing him with my robe.

He answered me with a kiss, a gorgeous kiss that made me want to fall to the floor and pull him inside.

"First, we eat," he whispered.

"Right, food," I said, feeling shaky as I took a seat at the breakfast table.

"So, you know we need to talk about things now," he

said. "Like real things."

"What kind of real things," I asked.

"Like when you are going back home."

"Home?"

"To Seattle, Shea."

His question took me by surprise. "I don't know. I'm not sure I should go."

"What do you mean you shouldn't go," he said. "Of course you should."

"But my family . . ."

"They have got this," he said.

"But you."

He reached across the table grasping my hand. "Where you go. I go."

"But you have a career too."

"Yes, and my career allows me a certain flexibility," he said. "If I have learned anything through losing you and finding you again, it's that I will always listen to my heart first and my fear second. What you wrote that day changed everything for me."

"What I wrote?" I said.

"I mean not right away. It was hard to accept but after that, you gave me strength. Losing you gave me resiliency and focus. Your note helped me decide to come back here and not give up on us ever again."

"I'm really not following you," I said. "What note, Troy?"

"I kept it," he said.

"Kept what?"

He got up and opened a drawer in the kitchen taking out his wallet. "The note you wrote telling me good-bye," he said. He opened his wallet and pulled out a folded piece of pale blue stationary.

I sat up straighter. I felt as though a cold stone were sitting in the pit of my stomach. "Show it to me," I whispered.

Troy handed me the stationary. I held it with shaking hands and recognized the notepaper. It was from a stationary set that Mom kept at her desk. She insisted we use it when writing thank you notes.

"When did you get this?" I asked. I was afraid to unfold the letter. I was afraid it changed everything.

"Paul brought it to me that day," he said. I knew exactly what day he meant. Troy sat down across from me leaning across the small table. "How long did you wait at the courthouse before you changed your mind?"

"What?" I felt dizzy and disoriented. My life story was being rewritten moment by moment.

His Three Piece Suit

"Last time you were here, you said you were at the courthouse waiting for me," he said. "What made you change your mind and send Paul with the note."

"I didn't," I whispered. I opened the stationary and read.

Troy,

I'm sorry I can't bear to do this in person, but it's over. I can't marry you. It would destroy my family, destroy our lives. I have made my decision and I need you to let me go. Please don't contact me. I know this is difficult but some things are for the best.

1+2+3—Shea

"One. Two. Three," I whispered.

"What do you mean you didn't write it?" Troy said.

"I'm so sorry, Troy,"

"But no one but us knew," Troy said. "One. Two. Three. I knew it had to be from you."

"I made a mistake," I whispered, wiping tears away with the back of my hand. "I told Paul. I told him about our secret signal."

"But your handwriting . . ."

"We used to take turns writing each other's book reports as kids. He knows how to fake my signature like nobody else."

"And Paul knew that I'd believe one, two, three."

"You didn't leave me ten years ago," I said, hot tears flooding my vision.

"And you didn't leave me," Troy said. He stood up and walked around the table, pulling me to my feet. He ran his fingers through my hair. "I am so sorry Shea, I never should have been fooled so easily. I always thought I shouldn't have left you without a fight, and now I know why. It didn't feel right."

"You didn't leave me," I whispered, my heart hammering in my chest. I had spent so many years feeling rejected and angry. My mind had a hard time processing this new information.

"Are you sure you were really going to show up?" I said, gasping and laughing. "You were going to go to the courthouse and marry me?"

"Yes, I was packing up to meet you. It had to be that day since Aunt Mayra had us booked for New York. My plan was to pack and leave a note just like you. But then Paul showed up."

Troy stared into the distance as if playing back a memory. "He was really flustered and I remember thinking it was because he was giving me bad news."

"He was giving you a lie," I said. "That's why he was

nervous. He was breaking us up."

Troy nodded. "I read the note. I said thank you. I didn't break down until I went back into the house and then I collapsed. Aunt Mayra gave me something to calm my nerves and the next thing I knew I was being packed up for the airport and I was back in New York City with my mother. I barely remember the flight home."

"And your mother certainly didn't want you pining for your summer romance."

"No, she did not," Troy said.

We sat in silence staring at each other.

"I think this is a gift," I said, softly.

"A gift . . . it was ten years, Shea. Because of Paul, we lost a decade together."

"Paul was just a boy too, a jealous boy that wanted to hurt us, and he did, but did you ever think that maybe just maybe we weren't supposed to get married that day?" I paused. "I mean is that the way you imagine it, running off to the courthouse and consummating our love in what . . ."

"I'd booked us a room at the super classy and always fresh King Arthur's Motor Inn," Troy said.

"You didn't! That place with the sign where that knight has an awkwardly big sword? Please tell me no." I covered my eyes.

"Um, yeah," Troy said, laughing. "I think we were able to request the themed round table room it was supposed to be a surprise. Oh my God, that's horrible isn't it."

I wrinkled my nose and shrugged. "If fate had brought us there that night, it wouldn't have been horrible. But, it's not exactly the way I would want to start the rest of my life with the man I love."

"We were just kids."

"Eighteen years old, we had no idea what we were doing."

"I don't know. I think we would have made it," Troy said, walking me out of the kitchen.

"Where oh where are we going?" I said, grinning as he led me up the stairs to his bedroom.

"Oh, I think it's time I show you that I may not be eighteen anymore, but I am still a lion in the sack."

He lifted me up and tossed me on the bed.

"Oh my, a lion? Is that so?" I said, untying my robe and laying naked on the bed.

He peeled off his clothes and crawled on top of me.

"If you growl I think I may never stop laughing," I said.

"Don't tempt me," he said.

"You realize that sources say you sexually peaked at

like nineteen. But lucky for you I am not even close to peaking," I said, playfully biting his lip.

"Oh science," he said, between kisses. "Well, I guess there is only one thing for us to do," Troy said, freezing above me, his voice suddenly serious.

"And what's that?"

"Practice makes perfect, baby," he said. I felt his hardness pressing against me. I spread my legs as he gently pushed inside of me.

"I'm just going to keep making love to you until we get it right," he whispered.

"If you insist," I said, sighing as he slid into me again, that familiar wave of pleasure building.

"This is where I belong," he said. The rhythm of his touch was hypnotic and intoxicating.

"We are exactly where we are supposed to be."

"Right here," he said, pushing in.

"Yes," I whispered. "Yes, yes."

And yes.

CHAPTER 19

I went home that afternoon to pack up for the drive back to Seattle. Troy had some work to do in his home office. He needed to explain to his partners why they had a 10 percent share in the winery across from Salishan Cabanas instead of 100 percent. There was a chance he might get fired, but he said the deal was locked.

I went home to have dinner with my parents. Dad had been officially discharged and the house was peaceful that night. Mom and I sat in front of the fireplace reading. Dad had gone to sleep early, exhausted after physical therapy.

I glanced at my phone. I was a little nervous for Troy and I was anxious to fall back into bed with him.

"Still no call?" Mom said, grinning.

"I'm sure he's fine," I said.

Just then, there was a knock at the front door. "I'll get it," I said, jumping to my feet. I stuck my head outside on the porch expecting to see Troy.

Instead, Paul stood beneath the porch light.

"Hey," I said, hoping I sounded neutral as a singular thought raced through my mind. Paul had stolen years of my life with Troy.

"Hey," he said swaying side to side, he looked nervous

chewing on his lip.

Ten years.

"I heard you were leaving tomorrow morning."

"News travels."

"Mom makes your business her business," Paul said.

"She does like to stay informed."

"Shea Marie," he said, softly. "Always the diplomat. I heard about what you did with the orchard, for your family. I heard how Troy helped too."

"How did you . . ."

"Ben told me," he said. "I feel pretty bad that I didn't figure out what was going on myself. I knew things weren't all right with Ben, but I guess I was afraid to question him, afraid he'd think it was a betrayal."

"I see," I said, thinking about the word betrayal. It sounded so interesting coming from his lips.

"The thing is I've been feeling pretty bad about something," he said, looking at his feet. "Something I did a long time ago Shea that I have to tell you. If I could take it back, I would . . ."

"I already know," I said, reaching out to squeeze his hand. Seeing him struggle and intend to confess, I felt as though a weight had lifted from my heart right there on that porch.

"You do?" Paul looked at me wild eyed. "I don't understand."

"I know what you did that day. I know about the note and it's okay."

"How can it be okay?" He said, tears filling his eyes. "I did it and the moment it happened I wanted to take it back but it was too late. Troy was gone and your family was so angry with you and then you left. I never wanted that. I felt as though I'd driven you away."

"I needed to leave this town," I said. "I needed to grow up and so did Troy. You didn't drive me away. I chose to leave."

"I'm sorry Shea. I'm so sorry for what I've done."

"And I forgive you Paul."

"You do?" he said.

I reached out and pulled my old friend into a big hug. "You were young too," I said. "We've all grown-up."

"Yes, we have," he said, leaning back, a slow smile crossing his face. "Thank you Shea. I feel lighter. I don't expect you to feel sorry for me, but it's weighed on me carrying that secret."

"It's time for us all to let the past go."

Paul nodded.

"Speaking of the past," I said. "You ever think of

going by the Gold Digger and visiting Celia?"

"Celia," he said. "Why would I . . ."

"Oh, I don't know, it just seems like she shines a little bit brighter when you walk in the room. I meant to tell you to call her that first night we went to the Gold Digger but things got so crazy."

"She shines brighter? Really?"

"She likes you," I said, arms crossed. "Seriously, how have you not noticed that?"

"I don't know, I just don't assume that women are falling all over me," Paul said, cheeks burning. "Maybe I should go get a beer," he said, backing up towards the stairs.

"You certainly should," I said, laughing.

"You're sure," he said, turning around at the bottom of the stairs.

"I'm sure."

"Like super-duper sure, like no doubt about it sure."

"Just get on out of here you goofball."

I went back inside and had just sat down again when there was another knock at the door. "Seriously?" I said. "I told you to get out of here."

"Did you now," Troy stepped out of the darkness into the porch light and my knees about gave way.

He wore tight blue jeans, a blue and black flannel shirt,

unbuttoned mind you, and steel toe boots and as I watched, he lifted a black cowboy hat and placed it on his head. This hat was proper and actually fit his head. Holy Moly I had never seen a sexier man alive.

"Hello ma'am," he said, "I was wondering if you might want to walk with me in the moonlight?"

I giggled. "You're a cowboy again."

"I'm not sure what you mean. I'm just me."

"You changed your clothes," I said, stating the obvious.

"I'm sorry," he said, pointing to the field. "I thought we could mosey on through these parts, listen to prairie dogs fight, light a campfire, and do cowboy things."

"Cowboy things," I laughed.

Troy held out his hand. "Will you join me Shea Marie?" he said, pulling out the stops with his fake cowboy drawl.

"Yes, sir," I said, doing a quick curtsey. I cracked the door open and shouted inside. "Mom, I'm going for a walk."

"It's ten o'clock," Mom said, poking her head outside. "Oh my," she said, a grin spreading across her face as she took in Troy's new gear. "Well, hello Troy."

"Mrs. O'Toole," Troy said, nodding and taking off his hat. "I'd like the honor of going on a walk with your daughter. I'll bring her back at a reasonable hour."

His Three Piece Suit

Mom just laughed. "Oh don't worry she's a big girl. You bring her on back any time you two please, now get on out of here."

We walked down the drive, hand in hand.

"You're a cowboy," I whispered.

He stopped and pulled me close. "I am a cowboy and I'm a suit and I love you."

We kissed and I felt that glorious rush of heat moved through my whole body. I wanted to kiss this man for hours.

"Make love to me under the stars," I said.

"With your Mama so close," Troy said, pretending to be shocked.

"My mamma is going to be surprised if I ever come home. Take me out where no one can find us. Make me yours."

Troy took me along the orchard path, well away from the lights of the house. We turned a corner and I gasped.

There was a blanket laid down on the ground like that first night he'd driven into the orchard. He'd added pillows and candles flickered in mason jars along a cinder block wall.

"Do you like it?" he whispered, looking at me.

I answered him with a kiss then pulled him by the belt into the center of the blanket and unbuckled his jeans.

"Lie down cowboy," I said. "Jeans off and get ready."

"Yes ma'am." He lay down on the ground and I wiggled out of my jeans and kicked my panties to the side.

"I see you mean business."

"Put the hat back on," I said. I hovered above him, my legs spread and dancing just above him. Then with a gasp, I slid him deep inside.

His hands on my back side, we moved together faster and faster until we were both shaking with pleasure, moaning and writhing as we came faster than ever.

"Wow," he said, his hand under my chin.

"You look good in that hat," I said, and lay down beside him, my head resting in the crook of his arm.

A shooting star gleamed overhead as it streaked across the night sky.

Troy kissed my forehead.

"I'll be your cowboy if that's what you want."

I rolled over.

"I love you as a cowboy. And I love you in a suit," I said.

"You are the love of my life and I love you for now and forever."

"Three words baby," he said.

"Three words."

His Three Piece Suit

"One. Two. Three."

Then Troy sat up and lifted me onto his lap again. I raised myself up and slid his cock deep inside, my legs wrapping around my waist.

Our bodies intertwined we made love on that blanket. The stars were a witness to our love. The apple trees stood tall as our guardians. The surrounding candles bathed us in a warm glowing light.

CHAPTER 20

Six months later

It was raining. One of those crazy sideways rains that come in the summertime and wipe away all memory of the blue skies the day before.

I waited in my little red Honda, engine idling just outside of arrivals at Sea-Tac airport. You're not supposed to park so I rolled forward every once in a while to avoid getting a ticket. My cell phone sat in the cup holder console. I kept glancing at the phone waiting for it to vibrate.

Instead, I looked up and saw him standing with his bags at the edge of the sidewalk.

Troy.

For a moment he didn't see me, and I got to soak him in as if he were a stranger.

His chocolate brown hair looked a little wild as if he'd just woken up. I wondered if he had fallen asleep on the plane. He wore a white t-shirt and blue jeans. He'd been gone for twenty-four long hours, a quick trip back east to meet with the movers and get the rest of his stuff packed up.

"No suit," I whispered, a slow smile creeping across my cheek.

His Three Piece Suit

Troy looked up and grinned at me setting his bags down on the ground.

I opened the car door and stepped outside leaning against the doorframe.

"Hey," I called, nodding his way. "You lost?"

Troy looked up at me and his face changed. There was a moment where he just stared as if he'd never seen me before. My heart seized.

I looked down at my pink sundress and my open toe sandals. I usually wore a pretty steady uniform of work out gear but Troy made me want to wear skirts and frilly dresses. I wiggled my freshly painted toenails knowing it would drive him mad when he saw I'd painted them cherry bomb red.

Sometimes I felt like I was a teenager again, except without any of the insecurity and drama. Troy was the longest crush of my life, eleven plus years and counting to be exact.

Troy picked up his bag and walked towards me like a man with a purpose. "You want to take me home?" he said, dropping the bag on the ground right in front of me.

"God, yes," I whispered. "I want . . ."

Before I could say another word, his mouth was against mine, his arm wrapping around my lower back. He pulled me towards his body with such force I gasped at the sexual charge.

The world around us grew silent.

We were in a bubble.

There was nothing but light and warmth and that rush of energy between my legs as his hands moved up my body. He held my face as he kissed me until he rested his forehead against mine and just breathed.

"One, two, three," he whispered. "One, two, three."

When we got back to the Holiday, I couldn't find a parking place so we ended up blocks away. It was pouring rain, but still Troy stopped me by the car. We stood in the rain making out. Troy's t-shirt totally soaked, we got so distracted kissing that we forgot his bags in the back seat.

"You look gorgeous," he said, running his hand along the lace of my dress.

"Thank you," I whispered, trying to drag him down the block.

"I mean it's a nice dress, but it could be improved."

"What?" I stopped and picked up the skirt. "You don't like it."

He laughed and pulled me close again. "I'm going to like taking it off your body one strap at a time," he leaned in, his mouth against my neck, nibbling at my ear. "I'm going to take you out of that dress and make love to you until neither of us can move."

"Oh my," I whispered closing my eyes. I could feel myself grow wet. "Now will you get moving, we are getting soaked," I said, pushing him down the walk and to the covered front porch of the Holiday. "You should have worn a jacket, Troy," I said, teasing him. "You look so hot in a suit."

"Less clothes, less bother," he said, pulling me into a passionate kiss. I turned to open the door and standing in front of the call box was a girl with wide green eyes and long brown hair. She wore a wrinkled white blouse and black pencil skirt. Neither of us had prepared for the weather.

"Sorry," I said, giving her an apologetic smile. "We haven't seen each other in a while."

"Twenty-four hours, twenty-four long hours," Troy said, his hands glued to my body.

"No problem," the girl said. She looked nervous and unsure of herself. She reminded me of myself when I'd first arrived in Seattle. I wondered if she were lost, then I noticed the vacancy side out front.

"You need inside the building?" I asked her, unlocking the door.

"I'm trying to get inside," Troy said, his hand on my back side.

"Behave," I said, swatting his hand away. The girl's eyes grew wide.

I mouthed the word "Sorry" and rolled my eyes. She was quite beautiful but there was something sad in her smile. I liked her eyes. She looked thoughtful and incredibly kind.

"I'm here about the apartment," she said, her voice shy and uncertain.

"Come on in, I'll take you to Billie." I held the door open for her while Troy kept a firm hand on my waist. It was hard not to be distracted by the fact that in a few moments we could be alone together. I couldn't wait to get that man in my bed. The things I wanted him to do to me.

The manager Billie had an apartment in the basement. Since the buzzer was broken, Troy and I escorted the new girl to Billie's door.

I knocked. "Billie . . . Billie the buzzer is broken. A nice girl here wants to move in. You should give her the apartment above me."

The girl with the green eyes smiled at me graciously. I think she liked having someone cheer for her.

Billie looked totally disheveled when she unlocked the

door. I wondered if she and Vincent were having some afternoon delight. The idea made me want to drag Troy upstairs even faster.

"You're in good hands," I said, as the girl stepped into the manager's office. "I hope this place works out for you. Come on Troy." I took his hand. "You have been a very patient boy."

"I have. I have been patient," he said, as we walked away. "I need some attention. Some one on one special attention."

"I know what you need, baby."

"Yeah, you do."

We took the stairs two at a time, almost running by the time we reached my apartment, 204. I pulled out my key but first Troy pinned me up against the door.

"I can't keep my hands off you," he said. I giggled and managed to get my key into the lock.

"Then don't," I said, pulling him inside my apartment.

We made a beeline straight for my bed. I fumbled with Troy's belt while he raised his arms up sliding off that wet white t-shirt. He spun me around and tugged on my zipper. His lips kissed the base of my neck as he unzipped my dress and dropped it to the ground.

Then he laid me on the bed with my legs spread. He

215

moved my knees together as he pulled my panties to my ankles and gently slipped them off.

He bent down and kissed me between my legs, breathing.

"I have missed this pussy," he said.

I laughed and swatted his head. "Oh, come on . . ."

"You think I'm joking," he said, sliding up my body. "I love every part of you."

"What about when I'm old and gray," I said.

"Especially when you are old and gray," he said, playing with my hair. "I will love all your wrinkles."

"Is that so."

"Will you love me when my balls are at my ankles?"

I laughed out loud. "That is horrifying, but yes, yes I will."

"Good because I will love you when this isn't new," he said, his voice growing serious. "When it doesn't feel like first love anymore."

"You will?" I said, looking into his blue eyes.

"When we're celebrating our tenth anniversary and then our twentieth, and you're sad because the kids haven't called like they should."

"The kids," I said, my mouth dry.

"I want it all with you. Shea will you . . .?"

His Three Piece Suit

"Don't," I said, my heart pounding. I'm not sure what I was afraid of but I felt overwhelmed and afraid.

"Don't worry," Troy grinned. "I'm not going to ask you to marry me today."

I sighed.

"I did that once, we did it the wrong way," Troy said.

"It wasn't wrong."

"It was. The next time I ask you to marry me, it will be the right time, the right way."

"And the next time you ask me, I will say yes," I said, looking at his gorgeous eyes.

"Three words," he said, rolling me on top of him.

"I love you," I answered with my voice and then I answered him with my body and soul.

CHAPTER 21

Five years later

The reunion was Odessa and Marco's idea. We landed at the airport in Puerto Vallarta and Marco had cars waiting to drive us to the hotel in Sayulita.

A man in a white linen suit held up a sign that read. "The Van Rossum Party."

I moved a little slower than usual, Troy's hand firmly gripped my arm as I slid into the back seat of the town car.

Those days I felt like I was eating for more than just twins. Mom had warned me that twins ran in our family and wasn't surprised when I'd given her the news.

I'd checked in with her before the flight thinking it would be over a week before we were back and I didn't want her worrying about me or the babies.

She and Dad couldn't talk very long. There was some reporter from *The New York Times* visiting the vineyards that day. They'd already interviewed Ben and Daisy and taken pictures of everyone including the grandkids.

"They want to know how a town like Salishan competes with the French," Mom laughed. "Can you believe it Shea?"

"Yes, I can, Mom," I said, rubbing my belly. I still got

218

a rush hearing the joy in my parent's voices when they talked about the winery. They were both so proud of the label and the business. The first year in competition and Dad's merlot had been rated at 90 points. A fact he shared with anyone who would listen.

"Shea baby," Troy called from the entryway. "We're going to be late."

"I got to run, Mom," I said, waddling through the house double checking the lights were off and we hadn't left anything on the stove.

"Don't eat any salads, and careful about the water," Mom said.

"Mom, that was Mexico like twenty years ago. My doctor says I just need to be smart."

"I'm just saying that your dad and I went to Tijuana once and I never left the bathroom."

"Mom, please . . ." I said, covering my mouth. "Knowing people go to the bathroom makes me want to barf. I don't want to hear about it."

"Sorry, honey, safe flight. Have fun with all your girlfriends and take care of those babies. I can't believe you're waiting to find out . . ."

"It's a surprise Mom," I said, picking up my purse. Troy poked his head in the front door again.

"We gotta go, Tell Daddy I love him. We'll send a postcard."

* * * *

And now here we were driving in the heat of Mexico on our way to see our very best friends. The villa was called Casa Flores and Marco had purchased the property as an anniversary present for Odessa. He said he had heard the tiny hotel was going to be demolished so he bought it since he was feeling sentimental. Troy and I laughed when we heard that. We were comfortable for sure, but Odessa and Marco operated at a spending level that included things like mega yachts. They'd just gotten back from a boat show in Florida where Marco had impulse bought a boat.

It amazed me how they stayed so grounded with all their money. Not that they hadn't had some rough years. Marco had testified against his father and the Mexican drug cartel. The truth was he had lost the majority of his fortune and then pivoted his business to pharmaceuticals, investing in companies that created cancer fighting drugs for children.

Odessa swore he was in the good drug business, not the bad. I just knew my best friend was happy, which mattered more to me than anything.

The driver pulled up in front of a charming white stucco hotel. Lanterns hung along a covered walkway. The sweet smell of wisteria and the salt of the ocean filled the air. I heard waves crashing in the distance.

Troy and I held hands and walked through the main building on a winding path past white stucco cabanas. I heard the sound of laughter.

The path opened up into a large courtyard with a large table in the center and strings of lights glittering overhead.

Odessa sat at the head of the table, her hair piled up on her head. She wore glittering earrings that flashed in the dark. Her eyes lit up when she saw us. She squealed and jumped to her feet.

"It's Shea. Shea! Darling!" she shouted running to me. Her hands on my belly, she leaned down to kiss my bump. "Oh, I love those babies. Your Auntie Odessa loves you. Look at you. You're gorgeous. Just gorgeous."

"Hello Shea," I recognized Callie's sweet voice immediately. She and Theo sat on one side of the table. Callie's head rested against Theo's shoulder, a soft smile on her face. She looked so happy and content.

I had forgotten to grab the magazine from the plane but there had been a major spread on Callie and her design firm. She and Theo had come to Mexico a few days early so she could check in on one of her billionaire clients.

"Hello stranger," Theo said, his gorgeous English

accent full of warmth. "It's been too long I'm afraid."

Theo hadn't changed at all. His long dark hair and pale blue eyes were still as sexy as ever. He and Callie had recently decided to spend half the year in England so their daughter could get to know both sides of her family.

Troy stood and shook hands with Theo patting him on the back. "Hello old friend," he said.

Marco returned from the kitchen carrying three buckets of what looked like champagne in his muscular arms. "And you're all here. Finally, my beautiful wife can stop her complaining. All of her best girls are here."

"Well, not all of them," Odessa said, pretending to pout. "Billie couldn't get away from the Holiday and Bella's in Venice."

"But we are here and that's all that matters," Callie said, her voice calm and soothing. I had always thought she had such a quiet gorgeous strength. "You have got the cutest bump, Shea," she said, staring at my belly. I wondered if it was hard for her to be away from her little one, or was she already yearning for another baby. Anabelle was almost two if I remembered right.

Odessa was the only one of us who hadn't taken the baby plunge, at least not yet.

Odessa raised a glass. "To friends."

Marco joined her. "To loyalty."

"To laughter," Callie said.

"To happiness," Theo said, looking at his wife.

"To life," Troy said, rubbing my belly.

"To love," I whispered looking at my beautiful husband and my gorgeous friends. "Always to love."

We clinked glasses and took a sip. I had never felt so blessed and lucky.

Odessa stood and took my hand, then she reached for Callie and the three of us stood together arm in arm, our heads leaning in together.

"Friends forever," Odessa said.

"Forever," Callie said.

I closed my eyes, inhaled and breathed in the scent of the sea.

The End

Want more Bedroom Secrets?

Get FREE BOOKS from the Bedroom Secrets Series

when you join my reader list here: **http://bit.ly/23bLXuc**

First you'll get a copy of "His Secret Love" followed by new titles coming soon.

SIGN UP TO JOIN EMMA'S READER LIST

http://bit.ly/23bLXuc

Learn more: **http://bit.ly/23bLXuc**

Thank You Dear Reader

Dear Reader,

Thank you for loving romance. If I could reach through the screen and hug you I would. Sharing my work with lovely readers like you is a dream come true.

Shea's story whispered in my ear the moment she walked on scene in "His Five Night Stand." She and Troy have always been my plan for Book 3. Spending time with the two of them in the town of Salishan, WA was such fun, there were a few tears as I raised that glass of wine and wrote "The End."

There is more coming too. Troy will get a chance to tell his story in "His Cowboy Heart." Stay tuned for release details.

This is also the part where I get to say thank you to all the wonderful people who keep me sane. First without my family I would most definitely lose my marbles. My sister, Olivia, is always my first and best critic. To my darling husband, Mr. X, you still make me weak in my currently sleep-deprived knees.

This book was written between late night feedings and school field trips. I love what I do, but if it weren't for the chorus of support from my amazing readers, I wouldn't be able to keep the fire lit.

You make it all worthwhile.

Thank you for being here.

XO to the moon
Emma
www.emmathornebooks.com

About Emma

Emma Thorne's approach to writing romance is that sexy + fun = happily ever after. She lives in Seattle with her smoking hot husband and their two children, a superhero of a little boy, and an adorable baby girl.

Emma loves connecting with readers and answers every email personally when the darling children allow. Find her online at **emmathornebooks.com** or reach out to her at emmathornebooks@gmail.com.

Read More by Emma Thorne!

http://amzn.to/1ZgnBKm

Printed in Great Britain
by Amazon

42428633R00131